W9-DJJ-025

The Man Who
Laid the Egg

The Man Who Laid the Egg

Louise A. Vernon

Illustrated by Allan Eitzen

HERALD PRESS
Scottdale, Pennsylvania
Kitchener, Ontario
1977

Library of Congress Cataloging in Publication Data

Vernon, Louise A
    The man who laid the egg.

    SUMMARY: During the early 1500's a young Swiss orphan
defies his guardians in order to study with Erasmus, the
Christian humanist whose desire for church reform grew from
his ideas on faith, reason, and education.
    1. Erasmus, Desiderius, d. 1536—Juvenile fiction. [1.
Erasmus, Desiderius, d. 1536—Fiction. 2. Humanists—Fiction]
I. Eitzen, Allan.
II. Title.
PZ7.V598Man   [Fic]   77-24939
ISBN 0-8361-1827-8
ISBN 0-8361-1828-6 pbk.

THE MAN WHO LAID THE EGG
Copyright ©1977 by Herald Press, Scottdale, Pa. 15683
    Published simultaneously in Canada by Herald Press,
    Kitchener, Ont. N2G 4M5
Library of Congress Catalog Card Number: 77-24939
International Standard Book Number:
    0-8361-1827-8 (hardcover)
    0-8361-1828-6 (paper)
Printed in the United States of America
Design: Alice B. Shetler

10 9 8 7 6 5 4 3 2 1

Contents

The New Learning

From the top of the stairs Gerhard Koestler listened to his two guardians argue in the library below.

"I tell you, Ernst, I'm fed up," Uncle Frederic bellowed. "The boy keeps his nose stuck in a book from morning until night. All he talks about is the new learning. Erasmus says this, Erasmus says that. 'Study Scripture but study Plato first.' What nonsense! It's enough to make me turn Lutheran."

Gerhard heard Uncle Ernst's smothered chuckle.

"At the monastery we have a little joke: 'Erasmus laid the egg that Luther hatched.' "

"It's no joke!" Uncle Frederic retorted. "In Basel people are wondering whether Erasmus is a Catholic or a Lutheran."

"My dear brother, have you made me walk from Mariastein in my monk's robe and sandaled feet to be told what everybody is talking about?"

"I sent a horse but you refused to ride it," Uncle Frederic snapped. "But no, it wasn't to discuss religious matters that I sent for you. It's about the boy."

The boy. Gerhard clenched his fists. *As if I had no name.* Uncle Frederic called servants by name, even Andreas, the lowliest serving boy in the castle.

What does Uncle Frederic have against me? Gerhard asked himself. If only he could somehow, somewhere meet Erasmus, sit at his feet, and find out more about the new learning. Christians should know what scholars have written about God and the Bible. But wasn't Uncle Frederic a good Christian? At prayers in the private chapel, his voice always rang out above the rest.

True, he had not given all his goods to the poor, or even to Uncle Ernst's monastery at Mariastein. Lately, instead of talking about his shipping business on the Rhine River, Uncle Frederic had been bragging about his new town house in Basel, his new horses with their fine trappings, and even expensive new books from Italy. They cost a fortune.

But I have a fortune, too. The castle. The rent money from the land. Then why did Uncle Frederic complain about expenses?

Andreas, the serving boy, darted up the winding

8

stairway. "Your uncles want to see you," he panted. He added with a mischievous grin. "I guess it's you. Your Uncle Frederic told me to go get *the boy*."

Gerhard's cheeks burned. Was he a nonperson to everyone in the castle? "You shouldn't eavesdrop, Andreas," he said in a stern voice, then grinned. After all, he had been eavesdropping, too.

In the library Uncle Frederic waved Gerhard to a highbacked chair at the huge, oval table. Uncle Ernst nodded a greeting. The shaved dome of his head gleamed in a ray of sunlight from the tall windows. Gerhard liked Uncle Ernst and more than once had thought of joining him in the Augustinian Order at Mariastein, but something always held him back. If only monks were interested in the new learning Erasmus wrote about!

Uncle Frederic fingered a heavy gold chain resting on the fur lapels of his new cloak. "As your guardians, your Uncle Ernst and I are concerned about your future."

Gerhard's hopes rose. Here was his chance. He didn't dare mention Erasmus, of course, but at least he could ask to study at a university.

As soon as Gerhard asked, Uncle Frederic scowled. Under his slanting green velvet cap, his heavy black eyebrows almost touched. "Your first duty is to fulfill God's will."

"Sir, I have studied very hard."

Uncle Frederic's scowl deepened. "Too hard on the wrong things."

"Sir, I've studied Latin, so that I can read the Scriptures, and—"

"Yes, yes. Very commendable, I'm sure."

"And Greek, too."

Uncle Frederic's mouth tightened into a straight line. "Why do you insist on learning such an abominable language?"

"It's because of the Scriptures, too. Erasmus recommends it."

"Erasmus, Erasmus, Erasmus," Uncle Frederic roared. "This nonsense has to stop." He slammed his fist on the table. "I keep asking myself where it all started."

"I found *In the Praise of Folly* right here in the library," Gerhard said. "It was my father's copy," he added softly.

Uncle Frederic closed his eyes. Was he remembering the 48-hour sweating sickness that had taken the lives of Gerhard's parents? Or was he objecting to *In Praise of Folly*? Maybe Uncle Frederic did not think people did the foolish things that Erasmus described.

"Uncle Ernst, didn't Erasmus translate the Bible into Greek so that people could read the original?" Gerhard hoped his uncle would say something helpful.

"Not translated but edited—and only the New Testament," Uncle Ernst corrected. "Erasmus will have to learn Hebrew if he wants to edit the Old Testament." Uncle Ernst gazed at the ceiling. "Erasmus didn't learn Greek until he was thirty."

Uncle Frederic cleared his throat. "Never mind that. If you want to study," he told Gerhard, "join your Uncle Ernst's monastery. Do your studying at Mariastein."

Uncle Ernst beamed. "As a matter of fact, Erasmus is one of us. He was an Augustinian monk at Steyn. Let's see; in 1492 he was ordained a priest by the bishop of Utrecht. Of course he doesn't wear a priest's robe now."

"You mean he's still a priest?" Gerhard's voice rose in astonishment.

"Yes."

"Then why doesn't he have to dress like one?"

"Special permission from the pope," Uncle Ernst explained. "He doesn't have to fast, either. Delicate stomach."

Uncle Frederic interrupted. "You know I can't stand that man. Why all this talk about him?"

"Because he's an Augustinian, like me," Uncle Ernst said in sympathetic tones. "Of course, being such a famous writer, he goes anywhere he pleases— England, France, Italy—because he has special permission from the pope."

"That's how I want to live," Gerhard exclaimed. "Go where I please, study at any university I want to." Why should Uncle Frederic mind? The expense would not be out of his pocket.

Uncle Frederic rolled his eyes upward. "In this life, it's not what we want but what God wants for us." He turned to Uncle Ernst. "It will be a work pleasing to God to persuade the boy to join your monastery. The sooner he puts on a robe like yours, the better."

Gerhard flinched. No one had ever suggested before that he become a monk. He had visited Uncle Ernst once, had gone down endless stone steps to a grotto where Mary's stone was enshrined. He couldn't remember what the miracle was supposed to have been. Perhaps someone had been cured of a disease, or perhaps the monastery itself had been saved from a threat of destruction. At any rate, the grotto seemed

11

like a tomb. How could anyone live cooped up near a miracle stone for a lifetime? Gerhard accepted, as everyone did, the idea that being a monk was a sure way to heaven, but to think of living as a monk day after day made him shudder.

"Patience, my dear brother, patience," Uncle Ernst said. "You must remember that I had a calling."

Uncle Frederic shrugged. "In the monastery the boy will be so busy fingering his beads he won't have time to worry about a calling or about Greek and those dead writers who are the basis of this so-called new learning." Uncle Frederic's voice rose. "I tell you, Erasmus and his ideas are to blame for all this unrest in the church. Now that I'm on the city council I'm going to see to it that his printer, Froben, moves out of Basel. I'll usher him through the city gates myself."

Uncle Ernst put his fingertips together. "We'd better decide about the boy."

"Uncle Frederic, I want to go to a university," Gerhard blurted out. "It won't be any expense to you."

His uncle toyed with his gold chain. A suspicion crossed Gerhard's mind. That new town house and all the other things his uncle had bought recently. Where had the money come from? Was the shipping business really that good? With a sinking feeling, Gerhard tried not to think about the money his parents had left for him. What was Uncle Frederic doing with it?

"There is no money to send you to the university." Uncle Frederic drummed his thick fingers on the table.

"But the rent money from the land?"

"Barely enough to feed the servants."

Gerhard stared at his uncle in disbelief. Uncle Frederic was not telling the truth. *He has taken my money.* Gerhard suddenly remembered something. Hidden in his tower room was a little pouch of gold coins he had collected as name day gifts. At least some money was left from his inheritance. Gerhard vowed that Uncle Frederic would never get hold of that pouch.

"It was your parents' intention that everything be given to Mariastein, after you enter there, of course," Uncle Frederic announced.

Another shock. Had his parents really intended that? "But I don't want to be a monk," Gerhard protested.

"Nonsense. What better life could you ask for? You'd never have to worry about where your next meal is coming from, and never be burdened with the cares of a castle like this. Besides, I can't keep running back and forth from Basel to look after it. Business hasn't been good in the last few months. On top of that, I have been elected to the city council, and I spend many hours a week at the city hall."

What was Uncle Frederic really saying? Why didn't Uncle Ernst say something instead of keeping his eyes downcast? Gerhard looked from one to the other. A slowly growing rage burned in him.

"You like to read," Uncle Ernst said. "You'll have plenty of time in the monastery."

"But who will teach me Greek?"

"Well, not Melanchthon. He's in Wittenberg." Uncle Ernst smiled a little as if to show he knew very well Melanchthon was a Lutheran.

"But I want to travel, to see the world."

13

"Whatever for?"

To be like Erasmus, Gerhard thought. Aloud, he said, "To learn about it and the people in it. Maybe I could meet Erasmus and find out more about the new learning." Gerhard regretted the words the minute they poured out.

This time Uncle Frederic pounded the table with both fists. "The new learning!" he shouted. "I don't want to hear another word about it or about Erasmus." He paused, and his voice dropped ominously. "You are going to Mariastein today."

Silence Or Violence?

Today? Gerhard sprang to his feet and stared at his two guardians in disbelief. "You have no right to do this. What about the castle, the money from my inheritance?"

"They will be given to the monastery for God's work here on earth."

"But—"

Uncle Ernst murmured, "It will please God if you go willingly and give up all your earthly possessions for His sake."

Gerhard saw that it was no use to argue. He would have to go to the monastery with Uncle Ernst.

"I—I have to pack," Gerhard blurted. He needed time to think.

"Of course, my boy." Uncle Frederic's voice was bland. "You may take along whatever you are able to carry."

Gerhard left the library, his thoughts in turmoil. He brushed by Andreas, crouched on the winding stone stairway. Eavesdropping again! How much had Andreas overheard? But that didn't matter. Andreas could not help now.

In the tower room Gerhard packed his books in two saddlebags and then remembered. There would be no horse to ride today. He'd have to walk with Uncle Ernst and leave the books behind. In just a few hours he'd be shut up in Mariastein forever.

Someone knocked. Had Uncle Ernst come after him already? But it was only Andreas.

"Do you want to go to Mariastein?"

"Of course not, Andreas. I want to study, to travel, to learn."

"Then why don't you run away?"

The idea was so sudden, so compelling that Gerhard caught his breath. How simple the solution! Excitement stirred Gerhard to instant decision. "What shall I take?"

"You can't take anything," Andreas pointed out. "Just walk out."

"As if I were taking a walk to think things over. You're right, Andreas. But how will I get past the gate-keeper?"

Andreas grinned. "You won't even see him. I know

a secret way over the wall. Come on. Your uncle is coming for you any minute now."

Gerhard had presence of mind enough to grab his pouch of gold coins and a copy of Erasmus' *In Praise of Folly*. He followed Andreas down the servants' stairway, so steep and winding that Gerhard slipped two or three times. Andreas hurried him through a tunnellike passageway and, to Gerhard's amazement, he found himself outside the castle wall. By this time it was late afternoon.

"Where will you go?" Andreas asked.

"I don't know. Maybe Paris, maybe Wittenberg," Gerhard started to say, but Andreas had disappeared. Puzzled, yet exhilarated at his new freedom, Gerhard headed for the village. How easy it all was! An hour before, he was a virtual prisoner. Now he was free to go wherever he wanted.

Gerhard walked through beech tree woods to the village of Flüh. The villagers stared at him. Was it because he was on foot instead of horseback? Did they guess he was running away? Gerhard quickened his steps, almost running past the houses with piles of hay and manure neatly stacked in front.

At the foot of the village he hesitated. The French border was only a step away. Should he go to Paris? On the other hand, the German border was not too many miles off. Why not go to Wittenberg and study Greek with Melanchthon, the famous Greek scholar?

Someone called his name. Gerhard whirled. Caught already? But it was only Andreas.

"What are you doing here?" Gerhard demanded.

"I'm coming with you."

"You can't do that. If Uncle Frederic finds out

17

you've left the castle without permission, you'll be punished. Go on back."

"Too late now," Andreas laughed. "I would've come with you before, but I went back to get some things we'll need." Andreas presented a bundle he had hidden behind himself. "Like your traveling cape and some food."

Gerhard felt a gladness he would not have believed possible. "All right, Andreas. You may come with me." He showed Andreas his pouch. "I've saved up all my name day gold pieces. We can live a year at least on these."

"Let's go."

"Andreas, does Uncle Frederic know I've gone?"

"No. They were still arguing when I left. Your Uncle Ernst wanted to wait until tomorrow and your Uncle Frederic agreed."

"Then we don't have to worry about being followed." Gerhard sighed with relief.

"Where are we going?" Andreas asked.

Gerhard made a fast decision. "Wittenberg."

Andreas stopped, wide-eyed. "Wittenberg? In Germany? That's where Martin Luther lives."

"How did you know that?" It had never occurred to Gerhard that servants would know about Martin Luther and his attempts to reform the church.

"The servants talk about him all the time, how he was a monk once and now he isn't, and how he translated the New Testament into the way we talk. Everybody knows about him, but why do you want to see him?"

"I don't. I want to go to the university there and study Greek."

"Why don't you go to Basel?"

"I couldn't do that. Sooner or later I'd run into Uncle Frederic."

"But Erasmus is living there now."

"What!" Gerhard turned to Andreas in amazement. What would a servant boy like Andreas know about a writer like Erasmus? "Who said so?"

Andreas grinned. "Your Uncle Frederic. I heard him tell your Uncle Ernst."

"No wonder Uncle Frederic wanted me out of the way in Mariastein. He hates Erasmus and the new learning, but I'm going to find out more about it from Erasmus himself. Andreas, we're going to Basel."

"Even though your uncle's there?"

"We'll just have to keep out of Uncle Frederic's way." Gerhard moved aside to let two horsemen from France go by. One leaned down and remarked, "You seem to be more than a peasant boy. could you tell us if this is the road to Basel?"

Gerhard pointed to the road out of the village. The other horseman looked at his companion. "We'd better find an inn for tonight. I don't think Erasmus would like to be awakened in the middle of the night even to hear about Berquin."

"Excuse me," Gerhard said, "did you say Erasmus?"

"Yes," the first horseman replied. "What do you know about him?"

Gerhard pulled out his copy of *In Praise of Folly*.

The other horseman whistled in astonishment. "It isn't enough that the works of Erasmus are read by scholars in England, France, Spain, Italy, Germany, and Holland. They are read even out in the country."

19

"I am going to see Erasmus in Basel," Gerhard blurted. Maybe these men would introduce him. "I'm hoping to go to the university there." By saying that, Gerhard hoped the horsemen would not think he was running away.

"Why don't we find an inn down the road?" one of the men suggested. "We can find out what people in Switzerland think about Luther and Erasmus." He invited the boys to join them.

A little later, Gerhard and Andreas stood in a hot, stuffy reception room of an inn. It was already filled with travelers. Merchants, sailors, farmers, women, and children laughed and talked. A bald and wrinkled waiter appeared. He spread a table and wooden bowls, wooden spoons, and individual loaves of bread. The babble deafened Gerhard. He could hardly eat the watery stew. Everyone else ate with noisy gulps.

The two horsemen messengers somehow steered the general conversation toward Luther and Erasmus.

"Luther slugs and Erasmus reasons," someone stated.

"Luther denounces and Erasmus ridicules," another added. "He describes the abuses of the church in such a way that you can't help laughing, but Luther wants you on your knees praying."

"But neither of them wanted the violence that is now going on—people being burned at the stake for their beliefs, or being drowned or beheaded."

Most of the people agreed that both Erasmus and Luther wanted to avoid violence.

"Then why are people still being beheaded or burned at the stake?" someone asked.

"Because that's the only way people will learn," a merchant snapped.

20

One of the French messengers spoke up. "Did Christ teach violence?"

For a moment everyone was silent. Then the babble broke out again. Some said Luther was not as violent nor Erasmus as gentle as commonly thought.

"Luther is a heretic," someone shouted.

The merchant pointed to the horsemen. "Let's hear what a Frenchman has to say about that."

The leader of the two messengers hesitated, then told how a man named Louis Berquin was threatened with death at the stake. "He's in trouble with Noel Beda, of the theological faculty of the University of Paris."

"What? What? Get on with your story?" several people called out. "Never mind names and titles."

The messenger went on. "Berquin has tried to show that Luther is not a heretic because he said the same things as Erasmus, who is not a heretic." He then explained that the idea could be reversed—Erasmus is a heretic because he says the same thing as Luther, who is a heretic.

Several people scratched their heads, or pulled thoughtfully at the lobes of their ears. Gerhard could see that few understood the threat to Louis Berquin.

"So what's the difference between Erasmus and Luther?" someone asked.

"Luther says, 'I cannot do otherwise,' and Erasmus says, 'I cannot be other than what I am,'" the second French messenger said.

"But it was Erasmus who laid the egg that Luther hatched," a man called out.

From the outburst of laughter, Gerhard realized that the joking remark was well known.

A sailor spoke up. "I travel up and down the Rhine all the time and I listen to what people say. Luther writes for the poor and Erasmus writes for the rich." The sailor pointed out Gerhard. "Look at this boy here in his fine clothes. I'll bet he's been taught his Latin and Greek."

Gerhard grinned and nodded.

"Take this other boy," the sailor went on. "I'll wager he never heard of Erasmus."

"Yes, I have," Andreas said. "He's a famous writer, and he used to be a monk. I mean he still is, but he doesn't wear their robes, and he lives in Basel."

At the sailor's crestfallen expression, everyone burst into laughter. As the talk continued, four armed men pushed their way into the reception room, accompanied by a fifth man in a fur-lined cloak.

Andreas tugged at Gerhard's sleeve. "It's your uncle. Let's go." He led Gerhard down a narrow, dark hall. Gerhard looked back. Uncle Frederic was holding a riding whip. "Where's the boy?" he thundered. "He's a runaway."

Silence greeted his words.

"Speak up, I say, or I'll thrash every one of you."

The two French messengers stood with folded arms. Other travelers huddled against the walls. No one spoke. Gerhard felt a rush of gratitude toward these strangers. In spite of Uncle Frederic's threat, they were going to protect him with their silence. *Threats and violence never work*, Gerhard thought. *At least they don't work in the right way*.

Andreas, with his expert know-how, found a back exit from the inn. The boys waited outside until Uncle Frederic stormed out of the inn, still shouting threats.

Uncle Frederic was holding a riding whip. "Where's the boy?" he thundered. "He's a runaway."

He and the armed men rode off.

The next morning Gerhard and Andreas rode to Basel with the two messengers from France. At St. John's Gate they joined other travelers waiting to enter the city.

"Why do you wish to enter Basel?" the gatekeeper asked.

"I have business with Erasmus," one of the French messengers said.

A bystander muttered, "That Hollander! Let him go back to Rotterdam where he belongs."

"Where can we find Erasmus?" the other messenger asked.

"At Froben's. Where else?" a well-dressed traveler volunteered. "He's there eighteen hours a day, give or take a few."

The gatekeeper asked the same question of everyone. Gerhard stated, "I want to go to the university."

Inside the city a group of people waited for the travelers. Monks, beggars, and businessmen stared at the newcomers.

"Where is the University of Basel?" Gerhard asked some boys about his own age.

A burst of laughter greeted him. Andreas doubled up his fists ready to fight, but Gerhard held him back.

"Where is the university?" a boy mocked in a falsetto voice. The others laughed again. "You'd better go back to the country."

Why were they so spiteful? Gerhard hadn't done anything to them.

"Leave him alone," another boy ordered. "Look at his clothes. Do country boys wear fine linen shirts and have their own serving lads?" He pointed to a building not far away. "The university is over there, hardly a stone's throw from the city gate, as you can see."

Andreas still wanted to fight. Gerhard stopped him. "Better silence than violence," he said. "Come on. Let's go to Froben's with the French messengers."

But the messengers had disappeared.

"Why didn't they wait for us?" Andreas asked.

"Their business is with Erasmus. Besides, we won't have any trouble finding Froben. His printing shop is famous."

A passerby showed them the way. In front of the printshop a serious-faced little boy with a high forehead was rolling a hoop. "Are you going in there?" the boy asked Gerhard and Andreas.

"Yes. Why?" Gerhard was amused at the little boy's earnestness.

"My father works in there."

"What is his name?"

"Johannes Froben. And my name is Johannes Erasmius Froben."

"Don't you mean *Erasmus*?"

"No. It's Erasmius." The little boy pronounced his name carefully.

It must be Erasmus, Gerhard thought, but he wasn't going to argue.

Erasmius stared up at him. "You think I don't know my own name, but I do. It means *the beloved*."

I wish my name meant that, Gerhard thought.

Erasmius bounced the hoop under his hand. "My name is Greek."

That could be the explanation, Gerhard agreed silently.

25

"Why are you going in there?" Erasmius asked.

"To talk to Desiderius Erasmus."

"He's my godfather, but you can't talk to him."

"Why not?"

"He's busy writing. Besides that, he's sick."

"What with?"

Erasmius rubbed the top of the hoop. "Kidney stones. When they hurt, he hollers so loud people in the street can hear him. Other times he talks so low you can hardly hear him."

Gerhard didn't know how to answer, but Erasmius didn't seem to mind. He prattled on. "He has a big nose, too, and it drips all the time. He has to use a handkerchief forty times a day." Erasmius looked down the street. His eyes widened. "Here come those men who were fighting here last week. I've got to tell Father." He ran inside.

Gerhard watched the men striding toward the printshop. It couldn't be! But there was no doubt about it. Uncle Frederic and his armed men were coming to Froben's. By the glint in their eyes and their determined steps, he knew they meant violence.

CHAPTER THREE

Doubly Beloved

Gerhard and Andreas darted into the doorway of a nearby shop. Several passersby stopped and craned their necks.

"What's going on?" someone asked.

Uncle Frederic and his men stood in a semicircle with their hands on their swords.

"Are those men going to hit someone?" a child asked his mother.

"Of course not. Basel's a peaceful city," she said,

hurrying the child down the street.

"It doesn't look very peaceful now," a man muttered. "Why would armed men come to Froben's printshop?"

"The leader's Frederic Koestler," someone exclaimed. "He's on the city council."

"What does he have against Froben?"

"It's not Froben he's after."

"Who, then?"

"Erasmus. Koestler wants him to leave Basel and go back to Rotterdam."

Uncle Frederic talked about ushering Froben out of the city, and all the time he knew Erasmus lived here, Gerhard thought.

"But doesn't he realize that Erasmus is making Basel the most famous city in the world? Besides, how does he know Erasmus is in the printshop?"

"Oh, there's no doubt about that," another man volunteered. "Erasmus works in there many hours a day. A friend of mine is his servant. He says Erasmus eats hardly enough to keep himself alive. Do you know what Erasmus eats for breakfast? One egg and some water boiled with sugar."

A number of people had gathered by this time. "He'll never be able to defend himself in a fight," someone said.

"There's another way to defend oneself," Gerhard found himself saying.

"What way is that, boy?"

"With words."

Someone exclaimed, "There's Erasmus. He's coming out of the printshop with Froben."

The crowd surged forward. Gerhard allowed himself

28

to be pushed ahead with the others. Somehow it didn't seem important to remain hidden, not with Uncle Frederic so busy confronting Erasmus. Would there be violence between the fighter with weapons and the fighter with words?

The first glimpse of Erasmus shocked Gerhard. What could this pale man with skin like parchment, thin lips, a nose like a bird's beak, and small blue eyes do against husky Uncle Frederic?

"A breath of wind could blow Erasmus away," an observer remarked.

"How foolish to raise weapons against such a defenseless man!" people murmured.

"Don't worry. Froben will take care of him."

Johannes Froben stood with arms folded facing Uncle Frederic. Froben's face was set with determination from his bulging forehead, with hair thinning on top, to his jutting underlip.

To Gerhard's amazement, without speaking a word, Uncle Frederic motioned his men to put up their swords. "Why do you insist on living in Basel?" he asked Erasmus. "Why didn't you stay in Louvain?"

"Because Basel is neutral ground. In Louvain I would not be able to avoid entering the arena against Luther."

"Ah, just as I thought," Uncle Frederic exclaimed. "You're a Lutheran."

"I didn't want to become a hangman." Erasmus shrugged his scrawny shoulders and held up thin, bloodless hands in protest.

Uncle Frederic stared at Erasmus for a moment. "Then you're not for Luther."

"No one can deny that Luther calls for many

29

reforms that are absolutely necessary." Erasmus took a handkerchief from his sleeve and dabbed at his long nose. "How strange it is that my silence against Luther is interpreted as consent, while the Lutherans say I have deserted the gospels."

"What side are you on, then?"

"The side of Christianity—a life worthy of Christ." Erasmus' weak but pleasant voice rose a little. "I don't meddle with other matters. I might add that I'd be made a bishop at once if I chose to write against Luther."

"Then you are for him," Uncle Frederic exclaimed in triumph.

"As you see, I am not a bishop," Erasmus replied.

The crowd laughed. "See how he holds his own," they said.

The laughter seemed to bother Uncle Frederic. Muttering under his breath, he motioned to his men and left.

"Andreas, follow me." Breathless with a sudden decision, Gerhard worked his way through the crowd until he stood in front of Erasmus. "Please, sir, my name is Gerhard—" He stopped. Better not give his last name. *Koestler* was already too well known.

"Ah," Erasmus said in his weak voice, "you have my name."

"Oh, no, sir. My name is Gerhard."

A slight smile creased Erasmus' mouth. "In Greek your name would be translated as *Erasmus*." He added, "It means *the beloved*."

Gerhard felt a glow somewhere inside. It was as if he belonged, as if he had a place in the world.

"More correctly," Erasmus went on, "it would be

30

translated *Erasmius*." He sighed. "I wish I had put my name in correct form in the first place. Too late, now. It is *Erasmus* to the whole world."

"Does your first name have a meaning, too?" Gerhard asked.

Erasmus smiled again. "Ah, that was a clever stroke on my part. In Latin *Desiderius* means the same as *Erasmus*."

"Then your name means twice beloved?" Gerhard asked.

Erasmus nodded, his blue eyes twinkling. "Are you here in Basel to study?"

"Yes, but my guardians want me to be a monk."

"Ah, you are packing your bags to enter the monastery."

"Well, no, not exactly." How could Gerhard tell Erasmus about running away?

"Let me warn you not to be too much in a hurry," Erasmus went on as if Gerhard were on his way to a monastery. "Don't let yourself down a well from which you cannot get out. Many enter a monastery for the wrong reasons. One may be frightened by sickness; others may be persuaded by parents or guardians who want to get rid of them, like yourself, perhaps. Still others think they will be saved if at death they are buried in robe, cord, and cowl. Besides," Erasmus added, "you have to have the body, the constitution for it."

"What kind of body do you have to have?" Gerhard asked, curious in spite of his firm intention not to become a monk.

"One that can endure fasting. I never could."

"What else?"

31

"The ability to go back to sleep when once awakened. I never could."

"What woke you?"

"The rituals," Erasmus sighed. "I detested them. I loved liberty and books."

Like me, Gerhard thought. "Why did you become a monk?" he asked.

"I didn't choose to. My guardians forced my brother and me into it." Erasmus sighed again. "You must excuse me. I must get back to my writing. I'm so busy I have no time even to scratch my ears." On the way into the shop, he looked back. "Come to my house for supper." He waved weakly toward a young man about twenty-two. "Hieronymus will tell you where." Erasmus made some joke to Froben, and laughing, the two of them entered the printshop.

"I'm Hieronymus Froben," the young man said to Gerhard. "My little brother told me he had already met you. I see you have interested Erasmus. He's always on the lookout for boys who are ready and willing to study."

Gerhard gulped. Should he tell Hieronymus his name? *If Erasmus finds out who I am, he may turn me away from his house.* Not the Gerhard part, of course. Again Gerhard felt the inner glow. *Beloved.* That's what his name meant, and really doubly beloved, since Erasmus was interested in him. An invitation to have supper with Erasmus! Who would have dreamed such a thing was possible?

"Maybe he won't like my name—my last name, I mean."

Hieronymus laughed. "Do you have a bad name?"

"It's Koestler."

32

Hieronymus sobered. "Was that a relative of yours who was here today?"

"My uncle. He and Uncle Ernst are my guardians, and I—" Should he mention that he had run away? Gerhard decided not to say anything. After all, he had enough gold coins in his pouch to pay his way. He wasn't a beggar.

Hieronymus was laughing. Startled, Gerhard stared at him. Was Hieronymus laughing about what Uncle Frederic had done?

"Excuse me, Gerhard. I was remembering how Erasmus first met Father in 1514. I was about thirteen then. You should hear Father tell the story. A middle-aged man came into the shop with a letter of introduction from the well-known Dutch scholar, Desiderius Erasmus. Father had already published *Adagiorium Chiliades* but had never met the writer. This stranger told Father that he was an intimate friend of the author, even looked like him, so he had been told. Any publishing arrangement would be as binding as if by the author himself. Of course Father wasn't deceived for a moment. He had Erasmus' bags picked up at the inn and Erasmus lived with us for many months."

Hieronymus apologized again. "Your talk about someone not liking your name reminded me of that." He told Gerhard how to find Erasmus' house and went back into the shop.

"Andreas, let's go to the marketplace and buy something to eat," Gerhard suggested. On the way they met the two French messengers.

"We got lost," one of them shrugged. "Basel's a very friendly city."

"We must not get lost again," his companion said. "Is this the way to Froben's?"

Gerhard pointed out the shop. What would Erasmus do about the news the messengers were bringing? If the church condemned a man as a heretic, no one could save him, not even a famous man like Erasmus. A shocking thought sprang to Gerhard's mind. To uphold the ideas of Erasmus could mean death.

At the crowded marketplace the thought was still with him. Andreas tugged at his sleeve. "We can't stay here. The city hall is right over there. Your uncle might see you."

"Not with all these people around, Andreas. Still, we'd better not take a chance." He reached for his pouch of coins to pay for some cheese. To his horror, the pouch was gone. All the money that he and Andreas were to live on had disappeared. How? When? Where? There must have been pickpockets in the jostling crowd watching Uncle Frederic in front of Froben's shop. What would he and Andreas do now?

"Leave it to me," Andreas said. He darted through the market shoppers and disappeared.

"A newcomer to the city, perhaps?" a voice murmured by Gerhard. "Maybe I can help you."

Gerhard turned. A monk with eyes gleaming under his cowl smiled at him. "You look bewildered, young man. Are you afraid of something? God sees and knows all that you do."

"I know that," Gerhard said.

"I can see that you are a promising lad, alert, and intelligent. The world offers many temptations. Why don't you come with me and have a good supper while you get your bearings here in Basel?"

34

At first Gerhard was tempted to accept. Without money, just how was he going to live? How would Andreas live? But instinct made Gerhard refuse the monk's invitation. He would have to listen to the pleas, the threats, the promises about monastic life, everything he was trying to escape.

"You have friends, no doubt?"

A trap. What if Gerhard named Erasmus? Even though Erasmus was approved by the pope, not every Catholic approved of Erasmus' writings.

Gerhard moved away from the monk. Where was Andreas? Why didn't he come back?

The monk glided to Gerhard's side. "My monastery is not far from here. We'll be glad to have you as our guest overnight. Perhaps we can have a little talk about what God intends for you, and why He has permitted you to arrive penniless."

"I didn't arrive penniless."

"Oh, then you lost your money here?" The monk nodded. "You see the evil ways of the world have already caught up with you. Fortunately, you have not sinned. You have been sinned against. Why not come with me?"

Gerhard could not stand the monk's talk any longer. He brushed past and hurried away, his one thought to get out of sight. Where was Andreas? What had he meant with his "Leave it to me." But Andreas was not to be found. Feeling more and more dejected, Gerhard wandered around until the idea came to him that Andreas would be in front of Erasmus' house at suppertime. Andreas would eat with the servants, of course, but Gerhard felt sure Erasmus's invitation included Andreas.

After a few false turns down crooked alleyways, Gerhard found the house. Andreas ran up to him with fear-widened eyes. "I knew you'd come here, but you can't go in."

"Why not?"

"Because your uncle and some men from the city council are there."

Gerhard groaned. That meant no supper, and he was growing hungrier by the minute. To think that he had run away from Uncle Frederic, only to find him more of a threat than ever. Why had Erasmus chosen to live in Basel? Why, too, had he chosen to call himself *doubly beloved?* Gerhard thought of his own name. It also meant *beloved*, but with everything going against him, Gerhard doubted its meaning.

"Where are we going to eat and sleep?" he asked Andreas. "We've got to find an answer to those two questions."

Andreas grinned. "I know the answer."

Gerhard waited. What was Andreas going to suggest?

36

CHAPTER FOUR

Unwelcome Visitor

Andreas led Gerhard down a side street and explained his plan. "All we have to do is become beggars."

"What! How could I ever beg? Andreas, it's unthinkable."

"You're hungry, aren't you?"

"Yes, but—" Gerhard shuddered at the thought of begging.

"It won't be so bad," Andreas said. "Lots of people do it. Besides, I found out who Erasmus' servant is. His name is Hilaire Bertulph, and every Sunday after church he hands out money to beggars. He says Erasmus has a soft heart for people in trouble."

"Why doesn't Erasmus hand it out himself?" Already Gerhard was imagining himself explaining to Erasmus what had happened.

"Erasmus is afraid of the plague."

"How can we live until Sunday?" Gerhard asked.

"Oh, I have food enough for us. We can sleep under bushes."

Gerhard did not ask where Andreas had found the fruit and cheese he shared. He did not object to sleeping under the bushes near the cathedral. By Sunday, with hair rumpled and his fine clothes dirty, Gerhard decided that he and Andreas looked like beggars. They waited by the stone wall overlooking the Rhine River.

"The people will be coming out soon," Andreas said. "They stand around and talk out here or by those trees. Hilaire Bertulph said we shouldn't be in a hurry. We're to wait until everyone has left."

"But Erasmus will have left, too," Gerhard objected.

"Not him. He likes to argue about the sermon with the preacher, Hilaire says. Afterward, Erasmus gives money to Hilaire to give to us beggars." Andreas grinned, his eyes full of mischief.

"But I'm not a beggar," Gerhard began, then shrugged.

Andreas laughed. "Who would believe you aren't?"

"Maybe I should try to talk to Erasmus and explain why we didn't come to supper."

"Better not," Andreas advised. "Your clothes are all dirty, and your hair is messed up."

"What's my book doing in the hands of a beggar boy?" Erasmus exclaimed. "Have you stolen it?"

In spite of washing their hands and faces at a nearby fountain, Gerhard could see that both he and Andreas looked like outcasts. By the time Erasmus had chatted with the preacher and started homeward, Gerhard was shaking with nervousness. He followed Andreas to where Hilaire was handing out coins to people with outstretched hands. Andreas edged to the front of the group. Gerhard ducked behind. He just could not force himself to extend his open palm. How humiliating it was to have nothing! Yet he could not let Andreas do all the begging.

Gerhard walked back and forth behind the group of people, trying to get his courage up. He noticed Erasmus standing at a safe distance away from the beggars. With a sudden impulse, Gerhard walked up to him.

"Sir, I—"

But Erasmus shrank away at first. Afraid of the plague, Gerhard remembered. Erasmus looked so frail Gerhard stepped back out of his way. The book he carried inside his clothes fell out. The copy of *In Praise of Folly* dropped at Erasmus' feet.

"What's this?" Erasmus exclaimed in his weak voice. "What's my book doing in the hands of a beggar boy? Have you stolen it?"

"Oh, no, sir. I've read it many times. It's my own copy."

Seeing Erasmus' interest, Gerhard poured out the whole story. Keeping a safe distance from both boys, Erasmus ordered Hilaire to take them to his house. "Tell Margaret to feed them and let them clean up."

On the way Erasmus seemed to lose his fear of contamination. By the time they reached the house,

Gerhard had told every detail of his running away and his hopes for a university education.

Erasmus took the boys into the kitchen. His housekeeper, Margaret, a robust woman with a huge white apron covering her ample form, curtsied.

"Margaret, feed these boys."

"Yes, sir. Of course, sir."

"They both need fattening up." Erasmus sighed. "They'll appreciate your good cooking. I wish I could more often."

"Yes, sir. Pleased that you say so." Margaret wagged her finger at Erasmus. "You know I always say, sir, if you'll just eat more milk and eggs you'd get over those stones."

When Erasmus left, Margaret whirled on Gerhard and Andreas. "All right, boys. You don't have to tell me. You've been living off fruit and cheese that you've snitched at the marketplace."

Gerhard was astonished. How could Margaret know that?

Margaret slapped down some bread and meat. "What do you mean playing on the master's good nature? Some sniveling story, I suppose, how you haven't eaten for days and you need money. Always money. They all want money, all the flock of beggars who traipse after my master, and he's so good-hearted he doesn't even know he's being made a fool of." Margaret slammed around the kitchen rattling plates and saucepans. "God's fool, that's my master. Well, don't think you can try anything around here, I'll feed you, because the master says so, but after that you'll get out, do you hear?"

"Yes, ma'am, and thank you," Gerhard said. He and

41

Andreas gulped down the food. After they had eaten, Margaret pointed toward the door.

"Out."

Had Erasmus meant that to happen? Erasmus had seemed interested in Gerhard's plans for further education. Gerhard opened his mouth to tell Margaret about Erasmus' interest. She picked up a straw broom and took a step forward.

A rustle down the passageway made her stop. Erasmus came in. "The boys can stay in that little room under the eaves," he told Margaret.

Slowly she let the broom fall to her side. "Yes, sir. Of course, sir." She motioned to the boys to follow her and led them up the winding staircase to the top floor. Muttering under her breath, she showed them the little room with two beds, dragged out some clean clothes from a little bureau, and told them to clean up. "Others have stayed here before you. They have studied hard. See that you do, too. You're not worthy of licking his shoelaces, but since the master says you're to stay here, I'll have to put up with you. That's not to say I like it. I don't, not one bit." Margaret flounced out of the room.

Later, Andreas got on Margaret's good side by catching some chickens that had escaped from the chicken house in the backyard. She let Andreas eat with her in the kitchen. Gerhard sat at the supper table in an adjoining room with other students and friends of Erasmus.

"Another one of your boys?" someone teased when Gerhard was introduced. Erasmus nodded.

"Your name is Koestler?" someone else questioned sharply.

Before Gerhard could feel uncomfortable, Erasmus began to talk about education. Gerhard felt a rush of gratitude. Erasmus knew Uncle Frederic was his enemy, but natural kindness overcame prejudice. *He doesn't hold it against me*, Gerhard thought. *I don't have to be ashamed of my name, no matter what Uncle Frederic does.*

"What should a boy study these days?" someone asked. "Grammar? Logic? The rules of writing precisely and to the point?"

"Rubbish, all of it," Erasmus said, pressing a napkin to his lips. "They all ought to be cleared away."

Gerhard listened in surprise. He had expected to hear about the new learning, but somehow he thought it was connected with the old.

"How old should a boy be before he starts his education in the classics?" the questioner continued.

"At age two," Erasmus replied.

"Two!"

"Yes. I told my friend Peter Gilles to implant the rudiments of Latin and Greek in his two-year-old son. What endearing stammerings the child would make in greeting his father in those tongues."

"That little boy will grow up to be a scholar," a visitor from Germany commented with a smile. "All German scholars are Erasmians."

"I hate those party names," Erasmus replied. "We're all followers of Christ and all work for His glory." Nevertheless, a person would be a better Christian, in his view, by knowing the classics.

"What about your own education?" someone asked Erasmus.

"Barbaric!" Erasmus retorted in his mild way.

43

"Ancient textbooks, dull drills. Still, one of my teachers, Johannes Synthen, had a certain degree of understanding about the classics. My father, too, had copied classic authors."

During the meal Margaret came to Erasmus' side and with flashing eyes announced, "That man is outside again."

Gerhard's heart sank. Was Uncle Frederic back?

"Why doesn't this pestiferous fellow leave the city?" Erasmus asked.

What an odd thing to say, Gerhard thought. Uncle Frederic wanted Erasmus to leave the city.

Everyone at the table seemed to know who was meant. It was not Uncle Frederic, Gerhard discovered, but a knight named Ulrich von Hutten, author of many tracts and letters imploring people to fight for a united Germany.

"Doesn't he realize gunpowder has taken the place of swords, lances, and spears?" people at the supper table asked each other.

"He mixes war with the gospel. He thinks Erasmus should show himself as a martyr, take sides, and fight to the death," someone explained. "Von Hutten is determined to stir up war against the Romanists."

Erasmus shuddered. "War? He and everyone else should know what I think of war."

A brisk discussion took place.

"Knights no longer have much power, not since gunpowder was invented," one guest said.

"Hutten hoped to start a *Pfaffenkrieg* (a war on priests) against Richard von Greifenklau, the archbishop of Trier. He wanted to control the Rhine River as a means of uniting Germany," another guest said.

44

"*The wisdom of the ages and the grace of the gospel will shape the mind of the child,*" Erasmus said.

"But it was a disaster."

"Yes, and that's not the only disaster. That loathsome disease Hutten has is enough to bar him from anyone's house."

The next morning Gerhard looked out his attic window. Below, on the street, a man paced back and forth. His shoulders drooped and his hands trembled. The wild glare in his eyes made Gerhard shudder. The man looked up. Gerhard could see the sores on the man's face. This must be Ulrich von Hutten, Gerhard decided.

Margaret, the housekeeper, came into the room. "Close your shutters!" she ordered. "I'm closing them all over the house." She looked over Andreas's shoulder and peered into the street. "Master will never be rid of him until the plague takes him."

"Is that Ulrich von Hutten?"

"Yes," Margaret snorted.

"Does he have the plague?"

"In a manner of speaking, yes. And he'll die of it, mark my words. Sinful man! Why must he drag himself to our door and persecute Master, who with one flourish of his pen can bring men's senses together without bloodshed or warfare?"

"But wouldn't a Christian help someone who's sick, like the Good Samaritan?" Gerhard ventured.

Margaret snorted again. "If you knew your Bible, young man, you'd know that you can't cast pearls before swine. If you do, they will turn and rend you. And that's just what von Hutten is doing."

"What does he want Erasmus to do?"

"To follow his violent ideas, that's what. He tried long and hard to get Master to fight, but Master was too wily to fall into that snare. And now look what has come of it. What if Master had joined forces with von Hutten? There would be war everywhere, to say nothing of the disease Master might get." Margaret glared at Gerhard. "What would a young one like you know about such things? Better not know anything about it at all. Just remember, if you sin, you pay for it." She bustled out of the room, adding over her shoulder, "If a person is not clean in body and mind, he's not living according to God's laws."

Gerhard puzzled about dirt and disease. Lots of people in Basel were dirty. He had seen them. True, most people didn't live long. Erasmus, in his fifties, in spite of his delicate health, his limited diet, and his painful attacks of kidney stones, had lived many years longer than most men. Did God send diseases or did people invite them? What about Ulrich von Hutten? Should Erasmus bring him inside and help him, like a Christian, or should Christians shun such people?

Gerhard had never thought about such painful questions before. The questions were like unwelcome visitors, and they would not go away.

CHAPTER FIVE

Two Sides of Truth

In the following days Margaret kept all the windows shuttered. Anyone coming or leaving had to go through the kitchen and out the back way. Whenever anyone passed the hen house, the chickens clucked.

"It isn't enough that Master is hounded by that man Hutten. The chickens aren't laying as many eggs," she fumed. "Besides that, who knows what important visitor has turned away from Master's door thinking no one is at home?"

Every day Gerhard kept a lookout after Andreas left for the parish school, an arrangement approved by Erasmus. One morning a well-dressed stranger came to the back door. Gerhard sensed Margaret's inner conflict. Should she be polite or should she brush the man off?

The stranger apologized. "I was told to come this way. I have come all the way from Italy to see Erasmus."

Margaret clasped her hands in front of her stomach. Her natural disapproval of intruders and her fear of being discourteous to an important visitor showed on her twitching lips.

"I fear these shuttered windows mean Erasmus has gone on a trip," the man went on.

"Yes, he is," Margaret said bluntly.

Gerhard was shocked. He had already learned a great deal about Erasmus. One thing Erasmus hated was lying.

"Ah, then perhaps you will let me just peek inside and see the chair and desk where the famous humanist does his writing."

"Most of the time he writes standing up," Gerhard volunteered.

Margaret hushed Gerhard with a stern glance but asked the visitor courteously, "Do you have a letter?"

Gerhard knew she expected the man to say no, but he brought out a folder in brocade embroidered with gold, green, and blue leaves and flowers. "Indeed I have a letter written by Erasmus himself. It's my greatest treasure." He showed Margaret the letter. "I've read all his books and my one wish in this life is to meet him in person."

49

By this time Gerhard was in total sympathy with the man. "You'll find him at Froben's," he blurted out boldly.

"Ah! How fitting! I shall find him among the scholars of the city. Thank you." The visitor hurried away.

Margaret whirled and cuffed Gerhard on the ear. "So the young one has taken over the house,eh? You ought to be ashamed of yourself."

"But Erasmus wants people to tell the truth." Gerhard rubbed his ear. It was the first time a servant had ever struck him, yet he didn't mind. Margaret was being loyal to Erasmus.

"Master himself says you have to be careful about telling the whole truth," Margaret said. "He has to be protected for his own good. As for you, go and see if that man Hutten is in front of the house spying again. If he isn't, go to Froben's and tell Master about this visitor."

The street was empty and Gerhard started out. He heard a rustle from the shrubbery. Ulrich von Hutten, his face covered with sores and his eyes glaring, sprang in front of Gerhard. "I know this is the right house. It's on Zum Lufft Street right by Little Tree Alley. Erasmus lives here, doesn't he?"

Gerhard hesitated. If he lied and said no, maybe Hutten would go away. The shutters would be opened and Erasmus and his friends could come and go without fear of being pounced on by sick people like Hutten. Gerhard remembered one of Erasmus' tactics. Erasmus never liked to be forced into saying yes or no. Instead, he sidestepped. Gerhard tried the same method. "What do you want?"

"I want Erasmus to acknowledge the great cause for which we are fighting." Hutten pulled out a sheaf of paper. "When the tyrants are expelled, we will see a glorious transformation. I have written a tract, *Against Tyrants.*"

"Erasmus isn't here," Gerhard said. That statement was true enough. Maybe Hutten would go somewhere else with his tract. But Hutten seemed eager to pour out all his grievances.

"Erasmus is a fame-hunter," he stormed. "At heart he is at one with the evangelical cause, but he has betrayed it. He agrees with Luther on many points. He can't attack us because he would be attacking his own writings." He raised a clenched fist toward the shuttered house. "Come out, Erasmus. Show yourself a martyr, ready to die for the gospel." Hutten clutched Gerhard's shoulder. "I saw you come out of his house. Go in there. Get him on our side. Get him to speak out once and for all."

Gerhard shook himself free and ran off. Hutten was speaking nonsense. Erasmus would never speak out for one side against the other, unless it was God's side. There Erasmus was firm.

"Wait! Wait!" Gerhard heard Hutten call. Again and again the hoarse call rang out. Housewives peered out front doors or upstairs windows. Gerhard slowed down and waited. This man was sick. Perhaps it would help to have someone listen.

Hutten limped up to Gerhard and pulled out a dog-eared letter. "Listen! Erasmus was my friend. Here is what he said about me: 'Is not his speech divine beauty and sheer charm?' Yes, this is written by the man who said my writings were elegant. He called me friend once. Why does he now close the shutters?"

In spite of himself, Gerhard felt pity for Hutten. What was the truth? Did truth have two sides? Was Hutten's truth different from Erasmus'?

Gerhard found out later what had turned Erasmus against Hutten. Dinner guests arrived through the backyard. Before Erasmus came in they discussed Hutten.

"Erasmus treasured Hutten's brilliant writings," one said. "He said so many times and wrote to people about Hutten."

"It was the letter from Erasmus that Hutten printed that annoyed Erasmus," another said. "Hutten tried to ally Erasmus with Luther, and that was bad enough, but Hutten wants to fight with real weapons, not just with pen and tongue. Everyone knows that Erasmus hates war."

The guests grew uneasy. Erasmus had not arrived. Had something happened on the way home from Froben's printshop?

"He always takes the long way around," someone said. "He can't stand the smell of fish on that little side street he could have taken."

"Erasmus has no sense of time," chuckled another. "He'd be late even with an hourglass in his hand."

A few minutes later Erasmus came in. He motioned the others to the table. Margaret hurried in with dishes of food.

"I dare not postpone my meal," Erasmus said. "My frail body cannot stand fasting."

Someone teased him. "I think there's only fish tonight."

Erasmus took the remark seriously. "My body cannot stand fish. For a long time if I ate fish it so disagreed with me that if I even touched it, my life was in danger."

When Hutten's name was mentioned, Erasmus sighed. "I don't fight with men of this sort. How deceptive are men's hopes. Why do people want to conquer instead of cure, suppress rather than instruct? The best Christianity is a life worthy of Christ. The truth may have to struggle but it cannot be overcome." Erasmus avoided speaking of Hutten until someone questioned him directly.

"Why won't you see Hutten?"

As always, Erasmus evaded a direct answer. "I cannot endure the heat of a German stove, and Hutten in his illness cannot do without one. We would be unable to find common ground on which to confer."

"Why can't Hutten see that he's not wanted?" one of the guests asked.

"He's unlike Luther's friend and colleague, Melanchthon," another said. "When Melanchthon came to Basel, he did not visit *here* lest it compromise Erasmus in the eyes of the Catholics."

Some thought Melanchthon might almost be considered a disciple of Erasmus.

"I've never collected disciples," Erasmus said, "or if I did I handed them over to Christ." He groaned over the letters he received. "I receive twenty letters a day and write forty," he joked. He would not answer a letter sent by a friend of Hutten's imploring Erasmus to see the man who had once been highly praised by Erasmus. Hutten had declared war on the clergy, and Erasmus refused to see him. "He's a quarrelsome brawler."

But there was more to it, Gerhard discovered. Pilgrims from France, Germany, and Italy came to see Erasmus, but Erasmus was always afraid of spies. "I am spied on by hundreds of eyes," he said.

Gerhard could see that if Erasmus admitted Hutten to his house, all the enemies of the Reformation of the church would want Erasmus excommunicated from the church. Hutten had written volumes against the abuses of the church, but he wanted to fight about them.

"Hutten has fortresses and walls, troops and guns, firearms and swords," Erasmus told people. "I exist only through the favor of the good and of a few powerful lords." He added, "I have no inclination to risk my life for the truth. It is not everyone who has the courage to be a martyr."

When someone asked what started the Reformation, Erasmus replied, "This tragedy arose from hatred of good literature and from the stupidity of the monks. If only they had let me alone and not tried to drag me into this." He said many times that each side heaped hatred on his head. "I belong to neither side. I fight against the excesses of both."

News came that Erasmus' books had been burned in Brabant.

"Who?"

Gerhard knew Erasmus was asking who would do such a thing.

"Hochstraten."

"Ah," Erasmus murmured, "my old friend."

"They say your books have been condemned by the pope."

Erasmus smiled. The pope had always approved his

54

work. Others, like Hutten, pleaded for Erasmus to take a firm stand.

Gerhard learned from the more talkative guests that Hutten had told Erasmus, "You turn like a weathercock. What you yourself sowed and planted, now you discard."

"He should have mentioned Erasmus' laying the egg that Luther hatched," someone chuckled.

"Hutten is just a rebellious hothead," another visitor declared.

"Yes, but he's one of the most elegant Latin authors of our time. Look at all the books he's written."

Hutten's latest manuscript was brought to Erasmus by Hilaire, the servant. It was an angry protest against Erasmus and was being passed from hand to hand in Basel.

Erasmus' table boarders were angered. "Hutten must be stopped," they said.

"But how?"

"I will be the sponge that wipes out Hutten's aspersions," Erasmus stated. He excused himself early from the table to write his defense.

"Erasmus has six fingers. One is a quill pen," one of the guests joked.

Erasmus spent much time on his "sponge." His weak voice quivered with indignation when he read portions of the manuscript to others.

"This will stop Hutten from writing anything again," everyone agreed.

But there was another way to stop Hutten that no one thought of. Gerhard heard the table boarders talking in low voices one evening.

"Who will tell Erasmus?"

"Perhaps it would be better to say nothing. You know he has spent much time writing his defense, and now it goes for nothing."

What was everyone talking about? Somehow, Gerhard could not bring himself to interrupt them. Margaret would know. She kept her eyes and ears open to everything that went on in her master's house.

"I don't know what it is." Margaret flung a wooden spoon on the table with a loud bang. "I'm fed up with these freeloaders, anyway, as if master had a mint of money. Of course money doesn't last very long with him, anyway. Three more shirts he had to have, and of course made out of the softest cloth. He can't stand anything harsh on his body." She glared at Gerhard. By this time he knew the grouchy housekeeper had only Erasmus' good at heart, and he could see that she was annoyed not to know what the table boarders were talking about in such hushed whispers.

"God had a hand in this," Gerhard heard one of the guests say.

Gerhard could not hold back his curiosity any longer. "What has happened?"

"He's dead."

"Who?"

"Ulrich von Hutten."

Gerhard gasped. Hutten was already a dying man when he came to Basel, and no one realized it. The news brought by messenger was that Hutten had died on August 29, 1523, on the island of Ufnau on Lake Zurich.

"What was he doing there?"

"He was seeking John Klarer, you know, the man who is both pastor and doctor. When the people there found out who Hutten was, they started after the doctor and he had to flee."

"Ah," someone sighed, "Hutten incited men to action all his life."

"And even in death," someone else added.

"Erasmus should not have taken such a strong stand against Hutten," a third man ventured.

"But Hutten never read it. He was already dead."

How strange and frightening it all was. Hutten had wanted the German states to unite instead of continuing as separate small states. He wanted people to read the Gospels that Luther had translated. He wanted to get rid of tyrants. On which side was the truth? Was it because Hutten wanted to fight that made his truth a falsehood? But if Erasmus had the truth on his side, why did he have to fight with words? Or did truth have two sides?

CHAPTER SIX

Secret Attack

One morning Gerhard found Margaret by the front door grumbling and turning a sealed letter over and over in her hands. "Who would leave a letter by the door like this? A messenger should knock, like any decent person, and hand the letter over saying who it's from. But this was so sneaky. It can only be a secret attack. Master has had them before." She turned the letter over several more times as if expecting it to tell her what was inside. Margaret had never admitted to

58

Gerhard that she could not read, and he didn't want to embarrass her. "Look at that seal. I've seen some like it on letters from nobility."

Gerhard recognized the seal. He had watched Uncle Frederic seal many letters with hot sealing wax pressed down with his signet ring. Uncle Frederic again? Gerhard had almost forgotten his uncle's threats, so much had been going on in Erasmus' house. With Ulrich von Hutten dead, there should be peace. But now it didn't seem likely. What kind of threat was Uncle Frederic making to Erasmus?

Margaret stared at Gerhard. "What's the matter, young one? You look pale. You're not catching the plague, are you? If so, I'll have you out of the house in no time, no matter what master says. But he'll agree. He's deathly afraid of plague. That's why he moves so often." She thrust the letter into Gerhard's hands. "You seem to know something about this, so speak up."

Gerhard read the address and received another shock. "This letter is for me."

"Come, come. None of your tricks. Who would want to write to a beggar boy like you. Give it back. I'll give it to master."

"No, no, don't do that." Gerhard was sure the letter meant trouble. "It's for me. Honest, Margaret. Look. There's my name, plain as day." He spelled out *Gerhard Koestler* with care. He didn't want to hurt Margaret by making her admit she could not read.

Margaret pursed her lips. "You'd best tell me what you know."

"I ran away from home," Gerhard blurted out.

"Where's home?"

Gerhard didn't want to admit that he lived in a castle. "Well, it's near Mariastein."

"A place near Mariastein, eh?" Margaret stared at him. "What's your name again? Koestler, is it?"

Margaret's shrewdness did not surprise Gerhard. He had only spelled his last name, not pronounced it, yet Margaret was saying it correctly.

She had another surprise for him. "You're the boy whose parents died and left you that castle."

Gerhard stared in astonishment.

"Oh, don't look so shocked. Things like that are known all around the countryside." To Gerhard's further shock, Margaret suddenly curtsied. "I could see right from the first that you were no ordinary village boy."

Gerhard grinned. "Don't ever curtsy to me, Margaret. Treat me the way you always have. I can't help it if I own a castle. Do you believe me now when I say this letter is addressed to me?"

"Yes, yes, of course. What does it say?"

Gerhard was careful not to break the seal when he opened the letter. "Dear Gerhard," he read. "You will no doubt be surprised to receive this letter, but I have my ways of finding out what I want to know. Since you insist on linking yourself with the archenemy of the church, Desiderius Erasmus, I have no choice but to turn over the castle and future rent moneys to the monastery at Mariastein. How grieved your dear parents would be to know their own son has joined this so-called reformer of the church. Your concerned uncle, Frederic Koestler."

Margaret sputtered in rage. "How dare he do such a thing?"

60

"He can do more than this, Margaret. My uncle absolutely hates Erasmus and all he stands for." Gerhard thought a moment. "I really am a beggar now."

"That's not true at all," Margaret said quickly. "You are nobly born. Nothing can change that." She added, "I always suspected it."

Gerhard could not resist teasing her. "How about Andreas?"

"Oh, him. He's my kind. We understand each other."

Gerhard was not sure about that when Andreas came home from the parish school with a black eye.

"What happened to you?" Margaret put her hands on her hips and planted herself in front of Andreas. Gerhard waited for his answer.

Andreas glanced at Gerhard with a sheepish grin.

"You've been in a fight," Margaret announced.

Andreas hung his head.

"More trouble for the master. He works himself down to skin and bones, even when he's ill, trying to make people understand Christian peace. So what happens in his own household? People he has befriended go out and fight."

"It wasn't my fault," Andreas said. "I was just coming down the hill in back of St. Martin's church and some boys jumped out from an alley and attacked me."

"You mean it was a secret attack and you did nothing to provoke it?" Gerhard asked.

Andreas looked at his shoes. "Well, I might have helped a little bit."

"All right, Andreas, what really happened?"

"Well, you know about the man, Oecolampadius, don't you?"

"The rector of St. Martin's?" Gerhard had heard that he was helping Luther reform the church. Like Erasmus and many others, Oecolampadius had Latinized his name, which was Johannes Hausschein, meaning *house lamp.*

"He's all for reforming the church," Andreas went on. "Did you know that when he started teaching at the university, they fired four Catholic professors?"

"What does that have to do with your fighting?" Gerhard demanded.

"Those boys said Oecolampadius and Erasmus are friends, and they said because I lived at Erasmus' house, I must belong to his side, and that means he's a Lutheran." Andreas paused for breath. "But they didn't know which side Erasmus is really on, because he never comes right out and says he's for Luther or against him."

"Go on, Andreas."

"They drew a line and dared me to cross it. And that's how the fight started."

Margaret sniffed. "I hope when you serve dinner tonight, no one notices."

Someone did, and that started a discussion.

"Who could bear to spend his life in a school among boys?" a guest asked.

"It seems to me an honorable task to train young people in manners and good books," Erasmus said. "Christ Himself did not despise the young. Young people are the raw material and harvest field of the nation. What better way to serve God than bringing children to Christ?" He added, "But my teachers destroyed my natural gifts with blows and scoldings."

Someone reminded Erasmus of his years in a monastery.

"I was totally unfit for monastic life."

"But you had a year's trial period. You were old enough to decide."

"Ridiculous. Who can expect a teenager to know himself? That's an achievement even for an old man. Who can learn in one year what many do not understand in their gray-haired years?"

"But a truly good man lives a good life in any calling," someone argued.

Erasmus agreed. "True. That's why I looked around to find out in what kind of life I would be least bad." He waited for the laughter to die down before going on. "I have spent my life in literary studies and I have associated with true followers of Christ. I resolved to live and die in the study of the Scriptures. It is both my work and my leisure."

One of Erasmus' friends began to laugh. "Do you remember about three years ago when that youth came up to you and said, 'I hope both you and Luther will become converted?' "

Erasmus smiled. He never laughed aloud, Gerhard discovered, yet was constantly joking. When someone asked him why he wrote so many books, Erasmus replied, "Because I can't sleep." He even joked about Luther. "My mind is Christian but my stomach is Lutheran," he claimed.

One day his servant Hilaire Bertulph delivered an anonymous letter to Erasmus. That night at the table, Erasmus told the guests that the unsigned letter demanded that he leave Basel, or the gunpowder stored in the city walls might be used for a better purpose than defending the city.

Was the secret attack made by Uncle Frederic? Gerhard couldn't be sure. He hadn't seen the seal. The attack only made Erasmus firmer in his views. The reforming of the church would not be helped by his leaving Basel. "How can a patient be healed by a doctor who is not there?" he asked. This letter was not the first to suggest that he leave. "If I go away to Rome, as some have suggested, the Lutherans will refuse to read me. The only way to cure the sickness of the Lutherans is by plucking it out by the roots."

"But might it not end, as it already has in many places, in frightful slaughter?" a guest asked.

Erasmus admitted the possibility. "The disease has gone too far for surgery."

Another guest pointed out, "In England the Lollards were driven underground."

"But not extinguished," Erasmus said. "Besides, England has a centralized government, not like Germany with its many small states. If the proper method to rid us of this evil is prison, exile, and execution, no one needs my counsel."

"But what can be done?"

"First, we should discover how this evil arose and offer immunity to those misled by others. Better still, offer a general pardon. If God pardons those who ask forgiveness, should we do less?" Erasmus asked. "I suggest that certain leaflets and books be restricted. Then all will breathe the sweet air of liberty as we do here in Basel."

Gerhard was not sure that liberty was sweet in Basel, not with secret attacks on Erasmus.

Watchful Waiting

The attacks on Erasmus took various forms. Gerhard found out that a doctor in Constance hung up Erasmus' picture just to spit on it every time he passed. A few months before, Erasmus, with Henry von Eppendorf and Beatus Rhenanaus, visited John Botzheim at Constance. Had the doctor met Erasmus there? Why would he become an enemy? Gerhard never found the answer but he thought more and more about all kinds of ideas—such as the church and what it stood for. Why were people so upset when someone like Erasmus tried to make it better? But then wasn't Luther trying to make it better, too?

People on the street discussed the unrest, read tracts, and took sides either openly or on the sly. Gerhard heard one man at the marketplace say, "Erasmus is an enemy of the gospel." Someone called out, "Who said so?"

"William Farel. Read his tract."

Erasmus joked about it. "I should make less of it were I to be kicked by a mule or a madman. Still, I prefer not to be kicked at all, as I have said before."

Many people claimed Luther had split the Christian world in two, and Erasmus had incited him by word and example. The old joke about Erasmus laying the egg that Luther hatched was still going around, but with more bitterness. "Why can't I be allowed to remain an onlooker of this tragedy?" Erasmus asked when discussions turned to the punishments, exiles, and executions of people trying to reform the church.

"I desire the glory of Christ," Erasmus declared. "On both sides I see things that displease me. From all parts of the world I am daily thanked by many who have never seen me, but know and love me from my books. Many have read Holy Scripture who otherwise would never have read it."

To those visitors who managed to coax Margaret into letting them in, Erasmus offered the same advice. "To learn about Christ, go to the sources. Pick the apple off the tree yourself. Christ desired that His mysteries be spread as widely as possible. I'd like to see the wives read the Gospels, the farmer sing of them while ploughing, the weaver remember them at his loom, the traveler recall them on horseback or boat."

If a visitor timidly suggested that Luther wanted the same thing, Erasmus said, "I acknowledge Christ. Luther I know not. I acknowledge the Roman Church. From this church not even death shall tear me. I shall not depart by a breadth of a fingernail from those who are in accord with the Catholic Church." He added, "If Luther had remained within the fold of the church, I would have rallied to his side."

"Ah, then you are against Luther, I see," a visitor would exclaim.

Erasmus would not admit any such thing. "Luther acted hastily, maybe, but certainly not with evil intent. Not every error is heretical. It would have been wiser, wouldn't it, to enlighten Luther rather than insult and irritate him?" Erasmus indicated that he would never live in any pronouncedly Catholic town nor in one that had gone over to the Reformation.

Gerhard watched, listened, and thought about the mysterious ways of life. There were always surprises. One day Andreas announced, "They want me to become a monk."

Gerhard stared in disbelief. Who would have thought Andreas' teachers would have suggested such an idea. "Are you going to?"

"Yes."

"But Andreas, why? Don't you know that's the reason I ran away? Otherwise, I'd be in Mariastein right now."

"Yes, I know that."

"Then why do you want to be a monk?" Gerhard demanded.

"To be saved."

They were talking at the foot of the stairway. Erasmus had just come in from a horseback ride, which he often took in the afternoon. Gerhard saw at once that Erasmus had heard what Andreas said.

"So you're young and burning with the desire for glory?" he remarked.

"Isn't it a work pleasing to God?" Andreas asked, a little uncertainly. Gerhard stifled a groan. He remembered that very same argument by his uncle months before at the castle.

"Not if you neglect charity," Erasmus said.

"Maybe I should go on a pilgrimage first," Andreas suggested.

"Worthless."

Andreas looked so crestfallen, Gerhard almost laughed. It was odd to realize that Erasmus himself was still a monk.

"Perhaps I should pray to the saints," Andreas murmured.

That remark really touched off Erasmus' views. "Praying to saints is foolishness and superstition. People think they will be preserved from disasters during the day if they look at the painted picture of Saint Christopher in the morning. They kiss the shoes of saints or their dirty handkerchiefs and leave their books, the most holy relics, neglected."

Andreas hung his head, looking as guilty as if he had been in another fight. This time, Gerhard realized, Andreas was fighting something in himself. Did he really want to become a monk, or was he simply yielding to other people's ideas? A person must learn to make up his own mind.

In his usual way, after seeming to be on one side of

an argument, Erasmus took the other side. "If you or anyone else wants to serve Christ altogether, go to a monastery."

"Should I be a monk or not?" Andreas asked Gerhard later, but was the first to admit he'd have to answer his own question.

"Maybe your teachers are trying to influence you, Andreas. Are they for or against Erasmus?"

Andreas wasn't sure. "They know he's still a monk and can hear confessions and that the pope approves of his works, but I don't think they like the way he criticizes the church."

Erasmus' criticisms gave Gerhard more food for thought.

"We hear very little about Christ in sermons nowadays," Erasmus complained. "We make Christian piety depend on place, dress, style of living, and on certain little rituals of candlelighting and chanting. It's an error to think religion consists of ceremonies." Then, in his typical way, he went on, "Yet I do not object to the ceremonies of Christians if approved by the church. They should not be done away with by enlightened men lest the weak be harmed."

Erasmus was never too busy to talk about education. A young father at the supper table asked him, "When should education begin?" Gerhard remembered what Erasmus had said another time, "At the age of two."

This time Erasmus said, "Not later than the seventh year."

"What do you think about private tutoring?"

Gerhard remembered his own private tutor with affection. He had introduced Gerhard to the works of Erasmus.

"Schools are better," Erasmus replied to the father's question, "but classes should be no larger than five."

"What about individual differences?"

"Very important." Erasmus was thoroughly convinced on that point, Gerhard could see. "An elephant cannot receive the same treatment as an ant."

"What do you think of visual aids to help learning?" the young father asked.

"They should be used, by all means. Quintilian suggested ivory letter shapes. I approve of pictures."

"I want my son to be a Christian."

"Of course."

The young father chewed his lip. "But how can I be sure he will be taught the right things? Patience, long-suffering, forgiveness, humility, self-effacement?"

Now Erasmus was in his element. Gerhard watched a glow come into Erasmus' pale cheeks. "There is no better way than through the study of the humanities and the Scriptures. The wisdom of the ages and the grace of the gospel will shape the mind of the child."

"But I'm afraid my boy will be corrupted in this sinful world."

Erasmus admitted the possibility, "That may happen unless he is disciplined by the classics and the Bible."

Erasmus was against bodily punishment. "Learning should be a delight," he claimed. "Play should be part of the school day. The purpose of games and exercise is to keep in trim for study. I often ride horseback in the afternoon to clear my head."

Schoolboys should learn good manners, Erasmus believed. Andreas told Gerhard later the rules Erasmus had told him.

"Like what?"

"Like not wiping a dripping nose on your cap or sleeve. That's only for peasants, Erasmus said, and he said some other things, too."

"Go on."

"Well, you're supposed to use a handkerchief if you yawn, and you're not supposed to laugh at everything, because that's silly, but to laugh at nothing is stupid," Andreas recited. "You're not supposed to guffaw so that it rocks the body, and your laugh shouldn't sound like a whinny of a horse, and you shouldn't show your teeth like a dog."

Gerhard could see how much Andreas had benefited from going to school and living in the house of a famous man. As for himself, Gerhard felt he was making little headway in his studies, and yet he studied hard, and Erasmus encouraged him to prepare himself for university training.

Margaret grumbled sometimes that he was bending himself double over his books. Sometimes she thrust both boys outside. "Walk. Exercise. The master says it clears the head." In good weather Erasmus himself went outside to a little summer house in the backyard not far from the chicken house. Here he would work on translations, or write letters.

Gerhard reflected on how strange it was that Margaret, who could not read or write, was necessary to Erasmus' work. If she, or someone like her, did not prepare the food, wash and mend clothes, and keep the house in presentable shape, Erasmus would not be able to do what he did best. But Erasmus believed housewives should read the gospel.

"Margaret, why don't you let me teach you how to

read?" Gerhard volunteered in the kitchen one day.

Margaret stiffened. Holding her head high, she refused. "I have no time for such foolishness."

"I hurt her feelings," Gerhard told Andreas later. "I guess I shouldn't have offered to teach her."

"Let me try. I know how to get around her."

Very soon, each evening at the kitchen table, Andreas was teaching Margaret how to read.

"What did you say to her?" Gerhard asked Andreas after the first lesson.

"I told her she could read the Bible for herself."

A visitor brought Margaret a New Testament. She displayed it proudly on a kitchen shelf until someone said in astonishment, "What's a Lutheran New Testament doing in Erasmus' house?"

From then on, Margaret hid the Bible, but Gerhard knew she studied it in secret. She did not let her reading skill interfere with seeing to Erasmus' comfort, and she did not change her habit of grumbling about everything from unexpected guests to the many gifts that kept coming. She showed Gerhard and Andreas the golden goblets, silver table service, and rare books Erasmus had received.

"Everyone in the world loves the master," she declared, "or if they don't, they should."

But somehow Gerhard felt uneasy. There was something in the air that he couldn't see. People in Basel were becoming more upset about the new kind of preaching that was being permitted. Was Basel becoming Lutheran? There was nothing to do but watch and wait.

CHAPTER EIGHT

Christian Enemies

In the little room on the upper floor of Erasmus' house, Gerhard slumped on the bed and stared out the window. "Andreas, take your nose out of your book and listen to me. What am I going to do?"

"Just keep on doing what you're doing, studying and helping Erasmus with errands."

"But I'm ready for the University of Basel, and now I can't go."

"Why not?"

"Andreas, I don't have the money, and I won't ask Erasmus for it. Besides, he isn't sure that I should study with Oecolampadius."

"Why not?" Andreas asked again.

"I don't think he and Oecolampadius see eye to eye."

Andreas grinned. "Maybe they see nose to nose. Oec's nose is as long as Erasmus'."

"Don't joke at a time like this, Andreas. I'm serious. What am I going to do next?"

"You remember what you told me when I asked you about being a monk."

Gerhard groaned. "All right. Don't rub it in. I'll have to answer my own question. I wish I could be in your shoes. You've made up your mind to be a monk and that's that."

"No, I'm not. I'm all mixed up. My teachers rave and rant against Luther and say he's not a Christian, but he put the Scripture into the people's own language so that everybody can read it. Why doesn't that make him the greatest Christian in the world today?"

"Greater than Erasmus?" Gerhard asked.

"Of course not, but why can't they be friends?"

The question haunted Gerhard in the coming months. He knew what Erasmus had said about Luther. "I would rather he handled the work of Christ in a way that he would be approved by the officials of the church." Erasmus surely thought Luther was a Christian. Or did he? "We should strive to instill Christ into the minds of men rather than fight with pretended Christians," Erasmus said. Perhaps he did not mean Luther but rather other groups of people protesting against the abuses in the church.

74

Gerhard and Andreas discussed the question many times. By diligent study, Andreas had earned a place in the dining room with the other boarders. "You will find a table set with learned conversations, not choice delicacies," Erasmus told each newcomer, but no one could fault Margaret's good cooking.

Again and again the subject would turn to Luther. "If, as appears from the wonderful success of Luther's cause, God wills all this," Erasmus said, "and He has judged such a drastic surgeon as Luther necessary for the corruption of these times, then it is not my business to withstand him."

Some visitors warned that unlicensed preaching in Basel would soon get out of hand. "Yes, we apostles of humane letters must walk backward like a crab," Erasmus admitted, when urged to take a stand.

"Why don't you testify," someone implored.

"I have testified openly, secretly, publicly, privately by my word, my pen, and my acts that I am unwilling to depart from the church by even a hair's breadth," Erasmus said, "I want to see the Christ of peace victorious. Instead, I see impostors, hypocrites, tyrants, and not a spark of the evangelical spirit."

One evening after the usual supper table discussion Erasmus said good-bye to his friends at the door. A group of Basel working men approached Erasmus. "We were wondering if you wouldn't say a word, seeing as how you know the Bible and all those dead men's writings. There's trouble brewing in Basel, and lots of people don't know which way to believe. The church says one thing and the Lutherans say something else. What do you say?"

"Go to the source, the Scriptures," Erasmus said.

"That may be good advice, sir, and I grant you it's an answer that should be taken to heart, but it's like a storm coming, sir. Nothing will stop a storm once it's on its way."

"Are you saying there's a religious storm stirring in Basel?" one of Erasmus' friends asked.

"Yes we are, and what's to be done?"

"The people must be reasoned with," the friend said.

"That won't stop people, if you'll excuse me for saying so. How can you reason with people who are stirred up like animals, you might say."

"What's threatened, my good man?"

"Why, our whole spiritual life. Who of us is going to heaven? We hear that Martin Luther says one thing, and other people say other things. Tell us, who is going to heaven?"

There was only one answer to that. Only God knew.

"The church says pay and you'll be forgiven," the leader of the working men went on. "Well, we've paid through the nose, so to speak, and I for one don't know any more than I did yesterday about whether I'm saved."

"Yes, yes, he's right," one of his companions said. "These Lutherans in the city stir up everyone. We're poor folk and not learned men. Tell us, is Luther right?"

Erasmus did not answer directly. "This worldwide storm has caught me unprepared. It has overtaken me when I was looking forward to a well-earned rest. Why thrust me into this?"

"We need a leader here in Basel," the working man said. "Is Luther right or wrong?"

76

"He has written much that is imprudent, yet it is not impious," was Erasmus' careful reply.

"Then what you are saying is that you're for Luther."

Erasmus made a guarded reply. "I know I've sometimes been accused of having a loose tongue, but no one ever heard me approve of Luther's doctrine."

"Then you're against him," the working men chorused.

"But we shouldn't adore a fragment of bread instead of God Himself," Erasmus continued.

"That means you're for Luther and his ideas."

But Erasmus had more to say. "I've never condemned the rites of the church. I have simply shown how they could be corrected, if misused."

The men scratched their heads, but went away satisfied when Erasmus told them, "Prayer lifts your soul to heaven." Erasmus explained to his friends that prayer was a tower beyond the reach of any enemy, but that learning armed the mind with sound principles.

After the working men left, Gerhard heard one of Erasmus' guests ask, "Why does Erasmus, for every opinion he utters, put something on the other side?"

"It's just his way," someone else said.

"Erasmus stands alone," another laughed.

Visitors came from time to time trying to make Erasmus admit he was an out and out Lutheran.

"How could I foresee that Luther was to arise and make bad use of my writings?" Erasmus asked. "How could I prevent him or anyone else from making wrong use of the gospels?" As usual he would add a biting remark about the church. "It's not by collecting the dry bones of saints that a man proves his Christianity. A Christian should order his manner of life in the Spirit of Jesus."

Gerhard noticed that in daily life Erasmus complained like everyone else about the cost of living. "It rises every day," he said.

Out of earshot, Margaret grumbled, "Master will have only wax candles, though he knows dipped candles are cheaper."

Gerhard listened to each in turn and wondered about the Christian life. Should a person who is following Christ's way ever complain? True, Erasmus was generous with his money. "It slips right through his fingers," Margaret said. "Master likes a good horse, a good servant, a good meal, and a good room. He told me so himself." She sighed. "It isn't the trickiness of bankers that does away with his money, though he would have me think so."

A friend of Erasmus was more explicit. "It wouldn't matter what Erasmus received, whether a pension by the archbishop of Canterbury, or from Lord Mountjoy, or from the Emperor Charles, he would always be in need."

When news came that Martin Luther had married, someone jokingly asked Erasmus if he would also marry. "I'm already married," Erasmus replied.

"What! Where? When?"

"My spouse is poverty and she's always with me." Erasmus explained that his books were his children. "Alas, they have not turned out well. I don't think they will live," he joked.

"What about your letters?" a friend reminded him. Everyone knew Erasmus wrote many letters a day.

"I write them only because my friends insist," Erasmus claimed.

"Then what about your poems?"

"I write them only to try out a new pen."

Sick or well, Erasmus always had a joke ready, unless something serious happened. A misplaced manuscript worried him. "What! Has the same thing happened again?" Erasmus told how in 1514 his secretary had mislaid a manuscript. "It was my poem honoring the marriage of Peter Gilles and his first wife, Cornelia Sanders. The nine muses praise the young couple. Its publication had to be delayed. Must I go through this again?"

That same year, he told his boarders, he had made the trip from England to Basel. In his handbag were manuscripts on the New Testament and Jerome, his lifework. Somehow the bag was put on board the wrong ship. "The labor of many years were apparently lost," Erasmus said. But the bag and the manuscripts were found on the other side. That had been an accident, but now one could never tell. Letters sometimes were intercepted and their wording changed. "My enemies throw stones at me every day," he said. They believed things he never said and took for the truth anything that was printed in his name.

The lost manuscript turned up after Erasmus had left the house. Gerhard took it to Froben's printshop. As he entered, he heard the creak of printing presses. The smell of damp paper and ink filled his nostrils.

A man pushed by him and addressed Johann Froben.

"You are Johann Froben, I presume?"

Froben nodded. Everything about his face seemed

79

strong, Gerhard thought, from his short, blunt nose, his jutting lower lip and strong jaw, and his domelike forehead.

"I hear you trained as a typesetter and proofreader under Johannes Amerbach, before he died."

"That is true," Froben acknowledged.

"And now you are a master printer."

To Gerhard the words sounded like an accusation.

"So they say," Froben agreed.

Gerhard smiled. The words sounded like Erasmus, who often said, "So I hear," or "So I understand," when any bit of news came his way.

The man pulled out a manuscript from under his cloak. "I have a manuscript here I want printed, and I want Hans Holbein to illustrate it."

Froben glanced at the title page. "But this manuscript is about Luther."

"Yes, he is the savior of our times," the man said.

"I cannot publish anything about or by Luther." Froben's words were as firm as his chin.

"Let me tell you something," the man said. "There will soon be a revolt in Basel, and you'll be sorry you didn't take the right side in reforming the church."

"The church won't be set right by being broken into fragments," Froben explained, "but by going back to the teachings of its founders."

"You think you can escape the revolt that's coming?" the man sneered.

"My part of the reform will be devoting my life and fortune to giving believers these teachings in accurate texts," Froben said with finality.

Froben's calm assurance seemed to impress the man against his will. He muttered something under his breath and slunk off. Gerhard turned over the manuscript. Froben took it in both hands, his face lighting up. "Everything that Erasmus writes receives the applause of learned men."

Gerhard thought about it later. Martin Luther was a learned man, too. He was a doctor of theology, like Erasmus. Why did two Christian men have to be enemies?

CHAPTER NINE

The Other Side

During the next few weeks Gerhard asked his boarders one by one why Erasmus and Luther could not be friends. Weren't they both doctors of theology? Hadn't they both lived a disciplined life as Augustinian monks? Hadn't they both spread the gospel— Erasmus with his edition of the Greek New Testament and Luther with his translation of the New Testament into the language of ordinary Germans? Weren't they both following Christ's teachings?

The boarders had different ideas. One thought Erasmus and Luther could not be friends because Luther had insulted Erasmus by writing to him, "Please remain now what you have always wanted to be—a mere spectator of our tragedy."

"But why is it a tragedy?" Gerhard asked.

"Because right is right and wrong is wrong."

"But aren't Erasmus and Luther trying to help the church?"

Another boarder spoke up. "Ah, that's the tragedy. It isn't a conflict between right and wrong but between right and right."

A glimmer of understanding came to Gerhard. People might have bits and pieces of truth, but God's truth was greater, and until they discovered God's truth there would always be trouble.

Several people thought that Erasmus and Luther could not be friends because Erasmus believed in freedom of the will and Luther did not.

"Some people think that as long as Erasmus refuses to write against Luther, they take him to be a Lutheran," someone remarked.

Another laughed. "They wouldn't say that if they could see Erasmus pull his cowl over his face every time he sees a Lutheran on the street.

The hundred streets of Basel were becoming more crowded every day, not only with Lutherans but with the followers of other leaders, each answering an inner call to help the church, each with his own idea of how the church should be reformed.

Margaret back from a trip to the market bustled around the house closing shutters. "There are too many people in Basel these days. I don't like it. I don't like it at all. Master is already talking about living somewhere else. He left Louvain because it was too Catholic, and mark my words, he'll leave Basel because it's too Protestant. When he goes, what will become of me?" Margaret burst into tears and covered her face with her apron.

"But Margaret, you'll go with him," Gerhard comforted her.

She uncovered her face and wiped her eyes. "I never thought of that." With a cheerful smile she went about her household chores. However, if anyone talked about Basel being in the midst of reform, she would snap, "Why do you say so?"

"Because of the outsiders coming in. There's Carlstadt and there's Ulrich Zwingli, to say nothing of Thomas Müntzer, William Farel, and Lefèvre."

Margaret shrugged. Gerhard saw that the names meant nothing to her. Too many people thronging the marketplace disturbed her.

A little man with a pale face and flaming red beard called on Erasmus. His name was William Farel and he talked wildly of reform.

Afterward, Erasmus said, "There's no arguing with Farel. If I had known what he was like, I would not have been at home."

Gerhard talked to Andreas about what they'd do if Erasmus moved away. Gerhard paced their tiny room at the top of Erasmus' house. "Andreas, I've been thinking."

"About what?"

"How two Christians can be enemies."

"You mean Erasmus and Luther?"

"Yes."

84

"Who said Luther was a Christian?"

"What more could a Christian do than give the gospel to people in their own tongue?"

Andreas was silent for a moment. "I don't know the answer, but my teachers at St. Martin's would say you are treading on dangerous ground. All you have to do is to obey the church and not argue."

But Gerhard wanted to think things out aloud. "Andreas, the church is just like a person. It can do wrong."

Andreas was horrified. "It's a sin to say such a thing. God made the church."

"Yes, but it's made of people, and people do wrong things, like selling pieces of the true cross and using the money for the church. Erasmus says if all the pieces of the true cross were brought together that have been sold, they would be a full load for a freighter."

Andreas laughed in spite of himself. Gerhard remembered how people said Erasmus pointed out the abuses of the church and made everyone laugh, but Luther had them on their knees repenting.

Gerhard heard Margaret calling his name in an irritated voice. *What now?* he wondered, starting down the steps. Everyone was touchy these days, almost as if waiting for a powder keg to be lit.

"Someone to see you," Margaret told him. She nodded toward the visitor in the hallway. He wore the full robe of a businessman and a cap that covered his ears.

Gerhard stared at the man. He looked familiar, but Gerhard could not place him. Was he one of the boarders who had eaten Margaret's good cooking just once or twice? Perhaps it was one of Andreas's teachers wanting to see about Andreas becoming a monk.

With an almost shamefaced smile, the visitor pulled off his cap and revealed a full head of hair. Gerhard was more baffled than ever.

"Don't you know me, Gerhard?"

Recognition came like a thunderclap. "Uncle Ernst! What happened? Why are you here? Where is your monk's robe and your sandals? You've got all your hair." Waves of uneasiness passed over Gerhard. Something was out of control. Had Uncle Ernst lost his mind?

"There have been many changes since I saw you last, Gerhard." Uncle Ernst clutched his cap and looked past Gerhard. "I've left Mariastein."

"But Uncle Ernst, you can't do that." The shock Gerhard felt made him stop and think. It was true that Catholics and Protestants in Basel argued about what should be used in a church service for the proper worship of God, but when dedicated monks like Uncle Ernst left their monasteries, what would happen to religion?

Uncle Ernst must have guessed what was going on in Gerhard's mind. "I'm not the only one who's changed inwardly and has come to see the truth."

Baffled, Gerhard could only echo, "The truth?"

"Yes. You see, in the monastery I was reading your Erasmus—"

"Oh," Gerhard interrupted, "and now you've come to meet him."

"No, not exactly. In fact, it was very strange. From Erasmus I turned to Luther."

Gerhard felt his knees weaken. He caught his breath. He knew what Uncle Ernst was leading up to.

"And then I had an inner experience," Uncle Ernst went on. "It was such a surprise. I never expected anything like it. I can never go back."

"You mean you are a Lutheran?" Gerhard gasped. The joke Uncle Ernst had chuckled at so long ago had come true. Erasmus laid the egg that Luther hatched.

"Yes, but that's not why I'm here." Uncle Ernst pulled out a pouch of coins. "Your Uncle Frederic sent this for your university fees."

It was as if the pouch Gerhard had first brought to Basel had been returned. But what had changed Uncle Frederic?

"There's a fiery preacher here in Basel," Uncle Ernst explained. "His exuberant preaching has aroused sleeping Christians, and your Uncle Frederic sees things in a different way now."

"Is the preacher's name William Farel?"

Uncle Ernst's astonished glance made Gerhard smile. "How would you know?"

"Everyone knows about him, and the other leaders, too."

Uncle Ernst shrugged off the other leaders. "Martin Luther is the heart of the Reformation, and I'm going to Wittenberg to see him."

"I'll go with you," Gerhard blurted out.

"You'll do no such thing, Gerhard. You'll stay here and go to the university. Isn't that what you wanted?"

"Yes, but I want to see both sides. Anyhow, the enrollment at the university is down to less than sixty. One of Erasmus' friends said that by 1529 there won't be a student left. I'll go with you to Wittenberg and study at the university there."

"But how can you explain this to Erasmus?"

"He and Melanchthon are friends, and I'll be study-ing Greek with Melanchthon."

With all the religious unrest in Basel, no one seemed surprised when Gerhard left with his uncle. By horse-back, by boat, and on foot, the two traveled to Witten-berg. Gerhard had never been bitten by so many fleas, eaten such poor food, slept in such makeshift beds, or heard so many fearful rumors in his life. The villages, one after the other, looked the same—small houses and a marketplace clustered around a rise which was crowned by the church.

By the time Wittenberg's walls came into view, Gerhard knew almost as much about Martin Luther as he did about Erasmus. Uncle Ernst told of Luther's ninety-five objections to the actions of the church, how Luther had refused to yield his convictions at Worms, and how he was kidnapped by friends and taken to the Wartburg castle. It seemed almost natural to Gerhard to walk down the main street of Wittenberg. The greatest surprise was to realize that Luther's home was a huge monastery at one end of the street, that Witten-berg University was not far away on the same street, that Melanchthon lived on that street, and that the church on the same side of the street hardly a mile from Luther's Black Cloister was the place where Luther nailed his protests to the door. How different from Basel with its hills and slopes!

"How will we ever meet Luther?" Gerhard asked. But it wasn't hard. He and Uncle Ernst joined a group of students from the university and came to the Black Cloister for an informal talk by Luther. Later, they lin-gered until Luther's wife, Katharina, invited the visi-tors to a meal. At the table, money was collected for her to pay for the food. Some paid; others did not. She didn't seem to mind.

A small man with large eyes and a hitch in his shoulder joined the group. Luther greeted him with a smile. "Sit down, Philip." Luther's small brown eyes twinkled. He stretched his head from his short neck and broad shoulders in welcome and spoke in a slow, melodious voice.

Philip. That can only mean Philip Melanchthon, Gerhard decided. The little man spoke with a lisp in a modest way. How strange that this man was considered second to Luther himself!

Gerhard hoped the name of Erasmus would come up during the meal. When someone mentioned Erasmus' name, Luther frowned. "Erasmus is an eel," he declared. "Nobody can grasp him except Christ alone. He's a double-dealing man."

Gerhard choked down a defense. After all, he was here to learn about the other side. The best way would be to listen.

"I've always given Erasmus the highest praise and defended him as much as I could," Luther went on, "but there are many things in Erasmus that seem to me to be incongruous with a knowledge of Christ. Otherwise there's no man more learned than he, not even Jerome, whom he extols so much."

Gerhard relaxed at these words. He hadn't really expected Luther to be that fair.

"I'm still debating every once in a while with Philip on how close Erasmus is to the right way," Luther went on. " 'Where is there someone whose heart Erasmus does not occupy, whom Erasmus does not teach? I speak of those who love learning. I ac-

89

knowledge his outstanding spirit, which has enriched my own.' " He added with a smile. "Those are the words I wrote him myself not too long ago."

Some of the students took notes on what Luther said during the meal.

"Everyone here is a Lutheran except me," Gerhard told himself later. He was glad he could see the other side for himself. He knew Luther was not allowed to teach at the university any more. Luther seemed almost like a prisoner in his own house. What he had started in the way of reforming the church was out of his hands. The egg Luther had hatched had turned into a monster.

Then the plague broke out in Wittenberg. People fled the city. Students left along with faculty. The horrible disease took its toll in almost every home. Martin Luther did not flee. He stayed and helped the sick. Gerhard stayed, too, but when Uncle Ernst died, Gerhard knew that he must go back to Basel—not to flee the plague as Erasmus always did but because he wanted to be a Christian humanist, someone who knew and understood the foundations of all Christian growth.

Storm Signals

On Gerhard's return to Basel, Andreas, with sparkling eyes, told him about the terrifying explosion. "The windows shook, and there were flashes and a terrible crash. A big cloud the color of ashes rose up to the sky. People armed themselves, ready for a fight between the Catholics and the Protestants." Andreas paused for breath.

"Go on, Andreas. What was it?" Gerhard could see that Andreas relished every detail of the story.

"Everybody was rushing around yelling, 'Stand to arms!' and other people shouted, 'It's the end of the world!' "

The cause of the explosion, Andreas explained, was that one of the towers in the city wall was used as a storage place for gunpowder. Someone had accidentally placed a number of barrels at the bottom instead of the top. A sudden summer storm came up and a flash of lightning touched off the powder.

"A lot of houses were destroyed and people were killed, too. Everybody thinks it's a bad omen. They say there'll be an uprising in Basel," Andreas said.

"What does Erasmus think?"

"He just said the explosion was due to carelessness."

Erasmus continued to complain about his many ailments—kidney stones, arthritis, gout, tumors, and ulcers. Hot weather undid him; fog made him melancholy, he detested wind in his face, heated rooms gave him headaches—but he never stopped his translating, editing, and writing. He forgot his own ills when Froben suffered acute pain in his foot.

"His right foot must be amputated," the doctors advised.

"Get Paracelsus," someone suggested.

"Why not Dr. Wonecker, the city physician?"

"He's been dismissed because he's against the Reformation."

The city council appointed Paracelsus as city physician. The many remarkable cures brought about by the most famous doctor of his time had followed him wherever he went. People stared in awe at the man with the high forehead, beardless chin, and piercing gaze. Although he usually wore his clothes until they were rags, in Basel he dressed better. Every month he had a new coat made for him and gave his old one away. Some said he was a quack. Students at the university called him a madman and suggested that he hang himself. But Paracelsus relieved Froben of the great pain he was suffering and advised against amputation. The praise of Paracelsus rang far and wide.

"Why don't you consult him?" a boarder asked Erasmus.

Paracelsus came once and said the kidney stone Erasmus suffered from resulted from crystallization of salt in the kidney. Erasmus, busy as usual, dictated a letter, "I have no time for the next few days to be doctored, or to be ill, or to die, so overwhelmed am I with scholarly work."

Erasmus thanked Paracelsus for saving Froben, "my other half," and hoped Paracelsus would remain in Basel.

"But when a man's time to die comes, no physician can save him," Erasmus' friends comforted him later that year when Froben died.

"I bore with calmness the death of my brother, but I cannot endure the loss of Froben." Froben had devoted his life to bringing the world the best literature. "When Froben showed me the first pages of some great author, how he danced for joy, his face beaming with triumph."

On the personal side, "Froben often paid my bills before I suspected it," Erasmus said. "He wouldn't take back the money. If my servant bought cloth for clothes, Froben would pay the bill."

It seemed to Gerhard that all the changes taking

place in Basel were pushing toward something in the future. Margaret went about the house with lips pursed and was more careful than ever to see that Erasmus' food was properly cooked, to have clean sheets on the bed, to see that no one drank out of the same cup at the table—a practice Erasmus didn't like. In paying attention to such details, Margaret seemed to push off old age and death.

"Master is drawing up his will," she told Gerhard one day with quivering lips.

Twenty-four shirts, five beds, tapestries, gold spoons and gold cups—all these and more were mentioned, Gerhard found out. Erasmus had already sold his library to John à Lasco, to be turned over after Erasmus died.

"He'll live a long time yet," Margaret insisted. "He has always fussed about his health." When Erasmus gave up the horseback riding he enjoyed for exercise, she asserted, "He'll take it up again."

Was Erasmus near death? Not at all, his friends said. Erasmus had said that for years and yet here he was, writing day after day as always.

"But my enemies never let me rest," Erasmus sighed. Henry of Eppendorf and Jerome Aleander, once Erasmus' roommate in Venice, now spied on him, Erasmus claimed. Eppendorf had corresponded with Erasmus, and later called him a coward. Now he wanted an interview.

"Mark my words, Eppendorf is another Ulrich von Hutten," Margaret muttered. "They worked together."

Erasmus' friends Beatus Rhenanus and Louis Ber came to the interview. Several other friends lingered nearby to overhear what everyone knew would be an attack. Gerhard joined them.

With shoulders stiff, Eppendorf presented a letter. "You wrote this to Duke George accusing me of heresy."

"That's not my letter," Erasmus said. "It's not in my handwriting and it's unsigned and unsealed."

Eppendorf made another charge and Erasmus defended himself again.

"Very well, I'll consider the matter and let Beatus Rhenanus know my decision."

"Otherwise, there'll be a lawsuit," Erasmus' friends told each other.

The terms Eppendorf suggested the next day irritated Erasmus. He was to write Duke George, explaining that Eppendorf was not heretical. Moreover, Erasmus must give a hundred ducats to the poor of Freiburg, a hundred to the poor of Basel, and two hundred to Eppendorf himself to give to the poor of Strassburg.

"I prefer to give Eppendorf two hundred ducats rather than have a lawsuit," Erasmus said.

"What the outcome of this will be I don't know," Margaret lamented. "His enemies want to see him penniless." Later, she said with satisfaction, "Master only has to give twenty florins to the poor."

Erasmus put off writing to Duke George. "No time is specified," he declared. "Besides, this man is inciting the Lutherans against me." He called Eppendorf a horseless knight, and pretended his coat of arms showed a hand with a dagger stabbing an elephant.

"I've had enough of such squabbling," Erasmus sighed. He politely responded to his enemies by letter, but ridiculed them in some of his writings.

Someone asked Erasmus why he hadn't joined Martin Bucer's church. Bucer was a Dominican monk and became a Reformer.

"My conscience wouldn't let me join," Erasmus replied. "If it could have persuaded me his movement came from God, I would have joined."

"But you see all these changes in Basel. The Reformation cannot be stopped."

Erasmus agreed. "But I see men who were fine men before joining the Reformers becoming worse. I've heard this and I've seen it myself. Besides that, the leaders oppose each other—the Anabaptists, Zwingli, Osiander, and Luther, to name a few. They should have made the gospel acceptable by their own holy conduct."

Gerhard listened to the endless discussions about reforming the church. Andreas, already living like a monk, rising early for prayers, going out to Mass daily, wouldn't talk about the changes.

"But can't you feel something is going to happen here in Basel?"

The old twinkle appeared in Andreas's eyes. "You mean like the explosion?" he grinned, then became sober again.

"There are storm signals everywhere," Gerhard said. "You're living behind closed doors already."

Andreas ducked, as if to ward off a blow. "Storms pass over, and if I'm living behind closed doors, it means I'm not opening them to the storms. Anyhow, none of the leaders agree among themselves, and they're all wrong. Why don't you become a monk? We could go to Mariastein together."

Gerhard stared at Andreas. What a strange path each of them had taken! The more Andreas wanted to be a monk, the more Gerhard thought of it as running away from the gospel.

"Maybe it's right for you, Andreas, but I want to know both sides, and even more than that. I want to know about the writings of great men in the past. You'll have to admit that the leaders in the Catholic Church aren't simple laymen."

"I don't want to be great. I want to be saved." Not long afterward, Andreas left for Mariastein, happy and bright-eyed about his new life of prayer and devotion.

Andreas is right, but I'm right, too, Gerhard decided. He struggled with his thoughts as if they were people. *It's not a fight between right and wrong; it's trying to decide between two rights.* Why didn't the leaders quit arguing among themselves and live according to Christ's teachings? As Erasmus said, leaders should not put stumbling blocks in people's way.

"Reforming the church will go from bad to worse," Erasmus said. "It has been wrongly handled. Certain rascals say my writings are to blame, but I've always declared that changes can be made without riots." He said the use of images for worship was at the best wholesome, at the worst harmless. He did not advocate doing away with the Mass, even though he deplored the money-grabbing priests. "If a new world could be built instantly, certain persons would not be satisfied. There will always be things that God-loving people must endure. Firmness and moderation can prevent bloodshed."

Gerhard discovered how serious the situation was one day on an errand to Froben's printshop.

Hieronymus Froben, now in charge, shook hands with a book buyer who carted away a load of freshly bound books by Erasmus. The man pulled the two-wheeled cart by hand toward the Rhine River. At the bridge he shifted the load and retied it, ready to climb the steep hill by St. Martin's church. Two men stopped him. Gerhard sensed a threat in their manner and came closer.

"Where do you think you're going?" one of the men asked the driver.

"To take these books to the rector of St. Martin's."

"Where did you get the books?"

"From Froben's."

"Ah, just as we thought. We'll start with these. That will show we want the Catholics out of Basel."

The driver protested. "But you can't take these books. I have to pay for them after I sell them."

"Who wrote them?"

"Erasmus," the driver said. "He's the most famous writer in the world."

"Erasmus is the one back of all this trouble," one of the men said.

The driver, with a troubled glance, pulled the cart toward the hill.

"Let's dump them into the river."

Several onlookers joined the group watching and listening. Gerhard felt tension growing in the pit of his stomach. The men had to be stopped.

"Wait," he called out. "The driver's not to blame."

His words acted like flame to a powder keg. With a shout the men forced the driver aside, pushed the cart to the side of the bridge, and shoved it over the edge.

"This is just the beginning," the man shouted as the

"This is just the beginning," the man shouted as the cart plunged toward the deep green water below.

cart plunged toward the deep green water below.

The driver, with head bowed, walked away. The onlookers silently watched him go. Then they murmured among themselves and finally drifted off.

The beginning of what? Gerhard asked himself. Why had an innocent man been subjected to an attack that was supposed to hurt Erasmus? Was this the first signal of a coming storm?

Fire in the Marketplace

Gerhard didn't mention the wagon incident to Erasmus. "I want to attack no one, provoke no one, even if attacked," Erasmus always said. He talked about his enemies. "They wag their venomous tongues at banquets, at court, in the confessional, in sermons, in travel carts, and in ships," he claimed. Basel was no longer a city he liked.

"Why don't you go to England?" a friend suggested.

"England is already responsible for my becoming faithless to my monastic vows," Erasmus claimed. "For no other reason do I hate Britain more than for this."

How could he say this? Gerhard wondered. Always before, Erasmus praised England and his friendship with many renowned men like Sir Thomas More.

"He's getting crotchety with old age," Margaret admitted. "He doesn't mean half of what he says or writes."

Gerhard didn't agree with Margaret's last statement, but he was puzzled by Erasmus' contradictions. How could a man who wrote so much about Christian living and a peaceful settlement between Catholics and Protestants be so upset over personal enemies like Eppendorf and Aleander? Shouldn't Christian peace start with one's enemies?

Erasmus called the Reformers pseudo-evangelists. "I am more nearly akin to the Anabaptists than to Lutherans or Zwinglians," he said. "They are praised more than all others for the innocence of their life."

Stories poured in from all sides about the execution of Anabaptists and others who sought freedom of worship. The innocent died for their beliefs. Why? Who made such decisions? Gerhard puzzled over the questions again and again. God permitted such things to happen. Did He want death for those who believed in Him?

The peaceful city of Basel, by decision of the city council, proclaimed freedom of worship. The Catholics could go to Mass. The Protestants could have their sermons.

"There will be no uprising here, Margaret,"

Gerhard told the housekeeper.

"People are never satisfied," she retorted. "I hear them talking in the marketplace every time I shop. They are saying the Mass must go, and the images of saints, too. Why can't they let good enough alone?"

Gerhard went to the marketplace to hear for himself.

"The Mass must be abolished," a man shouted to a group of listeners.

"But the evangelicals already have five churches."

"Not enough. Not enough," others shouted.

"What does the council say?"

In January the council restricted Mass to three times a day in Basel. In May, there would be a public disputation, when both sides could present their views.

"Too late! We want action now," people demanded.

The rumor spread that the Protestants in Basel would take matters into their own hands. Gerhard joined hundreds of men at dawn one morning in front of one of the churches.

"Get rid of the twelve Catholics on the council," they demanded. "The Mass must go."

"The council is in session," they were told.

"Why don't they hurry?"

All day the men waited. There was no sign of the council coming to a decision. The men armed themselves and gathered at the marketplace. The next morning, everyone clamored to know if the council was still deliberating. More people gathered, but still no decision was reached, although the twelve Catholic members of the council resigned.

"Let's take matters into our own hands," someone yelled. A roar of approval greeted him.

"To the cathedral!"

Gerhard felt himself shoved with others toward the hill. What was going to happen? The men wanted action. Which way would they go? There were at least three winding paths, not counting the feed-in lanes curving and folding in on themselves from every direction. Women peered down from the dormer windows of three- and four-story houses. At the cathedral doors, someone pounded with a stone. A priest came out and locked the doors behind him with a huge key.

"What do you mean locking us out of our church? We'll show you who has the right to enter."

The priest held his ground, hiding the key under the folds of his robe. The men muttered among themselves. Gerhard felt himself a part of it and yet detached. Were these men going to batter down the doors? They weren't angry enough yet for such drastic action, but they touched off a kind of courage in each other. *Why does it have to be destructive?"* Gerhard asked himself. Was it God who gave them strength? What drove people to destroy to achieve peace?

"Give us the key."

The mob pressed forward. "The key! The key!" others shouted.

"This is God's holy temple. You cannot have the key."

"Rid your church of painted images," a man called out.

"Or we'll do it for you," another said.

"God will punish you Protestants," the priest replied. With a sudden thrust, he dodged to the courtyard at the side of the cathedral and headed for a side door. The Protestants streamed after him and blocked his way. Step by step they backed him toward the stone wall edging the Rhine River far below.

"Give us the key. If you don't, we'll throw you over the wall into the Rhine."

The roar of the river seemed to echo the threat. The priest jumped up on the stone ledge and held the key before him like a cross. "If you come closer, I'll throw the key into the river."

"Then we'll break down the church doors."

"If you do, the city council will imprison you."

"No, they won't. They're all Protestants now."

The men advanced with cautious steps, one on each side of the priest and several from the middle. The priest waited until the last second, then flung the key into the river.

A roar went up. The Protestants milled around the priest.

"Throw him in, too."

"No, let's break down the doors."

The roar redoubled. "Yes, yes." The Protestants surged back to the double doors of the cathedral. Like a human battering ram, they pushed against the thick wood. The doors did not budge.

"We need a wooden beam," a man panted.

"Where will we get one?"

"They're building a house not far from here. We'll get a beam there."

In a little while the men came back with a heavy beam. From a nearby fountain Gerhard watched the men line up on each side and swing the beam back and forth. He dreaded hearing the crunch of destruction, yet he was fascinated with the actions of men intent on destroying what belonged to God. He barely had time to think how foolish these men were when the doors began to give way. A second time, a third time the men ran the beam against the doors. The doors burst open and with a high-pitched yell the mob swarmed into the dark interior of the cathedral.

Gerhard followed, drawn by a force he could not explain. Ahead of him men leaped on the altar, slashed the gold cloths, ripped down embroidered hangings, toppled statues of the Virgin Mary and the Christ child, of the saints and of Jesus on the cross. Some seized gold candlesticks and knocked out stained glass windows.

"Burn them up! Burn everything?"

"Not here, not here! To the marketplace."

With yells of approval, the Protestants seized statues and paintings. Some hurried down the sloping path in front of the cathedral; others followed the road past St. Martin's church. In the marketplace they heaped up the rubble.

Gerhard joined others who were watching the piles grow higher. A silence had come over the Protestants.

"What good is all this doing?" one of the spectators ventured.

"We'll give the wood to the poor," a Protestant said.

"Yes, yes. Help the poor. That's what God wants," others chimed in.

The poor people of Basel did not need a second invitation. They clawed over the pieces. Women stuffed their aprons with chunks of painted wood, quarreled with each other over the biggest pieces, and complained in bitter tones about their neighbors getting more.

The city council ordered the rubble burned. The fire

106

lasted two days and two nights.

"Happily, no blood was shed," Erasmus observed. "It's surprising that no miracle occurred, considering how many used to occur whenever the saints were even slightly offended."

Margaret overheard him. "How master can joke about this, I don't know," she told Gerhard.

Gerhard wondered, too. Erasmus made people laugh with his biting wit. Maybe if he had seen the mob at work he wouldn't have joked. But Erasmus always kept to the sidelines as a spectator. But what would the world be without an Erasmus to point out human folly?

Those who ate at Erasmus' table had more to talk about than ever.

"Now that Basel is reformed, will he still remain here?" someone asked.

Another recalled that when Erasmus was living in Louvain, the Catholics wanted him to write against Luther. Now in Basel, the Evangelicals wanted him to stay.

"But why? Erasmus is still a Catholic."

"The Evangelicals say if he weren't of the same mind as the Reformers, he'd have left Basel long ago. Erasmus is so renowned that many people who are hesitating about the reforming of the church would join the Evangelicals."

When someone asked Erasmus what he thought about the changes in Basel, he admitted, "Life is unbearable here. Better to live among the Turks than amid such contention."

Where could he go? He had invitations from England, France, Hungary, and Poland, to name a few.

"Poland?" someone questioned.

"Yes, indeed. Many Polish students, speaking Latin, of course, have come to Basel to study."

"But the university has been suspended now," one of the guests stated. "Oecolampadius is now the main minister at the cathedral."

"He and Erasmus were friends once, weren't they?" someone asked after Erasmus left the table one night.

"Yes, and now here he is, a living corpse, so Boniface Amerbach says, with trembling head and body. He's younger than Erasmus and yet he's an old man."

The question the guests asked was whether Erasmus and Oecolampadius would agree, now that Oecolampadius was the head of the new religious movement in Basel. Erasmus said that the opinions of Oecolampadius would not displease him except for the fact that they were contrary to the consensus of the church.

Once again the conjectures mounted. Would Erasmus stay in Basel or wouldn't he? Was he for or against the Reformers?

"I would like a drink from the waters of the Tiber," Erasmus mused.

"Ah, then, he wants to live in Rome," his friends said.

"I love no people more than the French," Erasmus added.

"Aha, he wants to live in Paris, where he once studied," his friends decided. But there was too much warfare going on there.

Then what about the Netherlands? After all, Erasmus signed many of his letters *Erasmus of Rotterdam*.

"What about Spain?"

"No, he never liked it," Erasmus' friends said.

"He can't go far, wherever he goes," Margaret told Gerhard.

"Wherever I go, it will be at the risk of my life," Erasmus said, "but I am leaving Basel."

CHAPTER TWELVE

Citizen of the World

Did Erasmus mean what he said? Was he really leaving? No one was quite sure. Erasmus hedged and murmured, complaining of not being well enough to go anywhere and at the same time asking Margaret to pack for his journey.

"Is he leaving or isn't he?" Gerhard asked her.

"I don't know. I'm packing, and his servant is packing." She looked at Gerhard with a slight frown. "What will you do when he leaves?"

"Go with him." For a long time Gerhard had watched and listened to the various secretaries Erasmus dictated to. They would come and go. Some were still students. Some were scholars who worked at Froben's. From his own studies in Latin, and hearing Latin spoken daily, Gerhard had become familiar with the rhythm of Erasmus' writing.

"You mean you would be a secretary for him?" Margaret asked.

"Why not? Don't you think I know enough?"

Margaret put her hands on her hips. "You've been here a long time. I've wondered why you hadn't spoken to master long before this. I hope you won't be like that Charles van Uutenhoven last year."

Gerhard remembered Charles, a young man interested in the Reformation but not inclined to study. After a few months he left without warning for Padua. "But he wasn't a secretary, Margaret."

"Yes, yes, I remember that now. I was thinking of Nicholas Cannius."

Cannius had been one of Erasmus' secretaries but had quarreled with the master. Cannius, too, had left, like many others, some friendly, some not. Many wanted to meet a famous man, to reflect in his glory, to boast that they knew Erasmus.

"Sometimes I think the master would rather be by himself," Margaret said, "but of course he has to have someone look after him."

With just a few bags packed, Erasmus left one day with his servant.

"Where was he going, Margaret? Didn't he tell you?" Gerhard asked.

"The Netherlands. But I'm sure he'll be back."

111

In a short time Erasmus returned. "Kidney stones," he told the household. His face was white and pinched with pain. Later he started out again.

"Where to this time?" his friends asked Margaret.

"He says Rome. But mark my words, he'll be back."

This time Erasmus got as far as Constance before he returned to Basel.

"What's he going to do now?" everyone asked. "He can't go far."

"But he insists on going."

Erasmus chose Freiburg in Breisgau, not far from Basel, but in the territory of Archduke Ferdinand, who had invited him to live in Vienna.

"If only the Reformers had not stormed the churches," Erasmus' friends groaned. The cathedral was not the only place that had been desecrated, as Gerhard found out. "Erasmus would have stayed here."

"When is he leaving for Freiburg?"

No one really knew, but this time the packing of Erasmus' belongings was in earnest. Everything down to the chickens in the coop were either sent ahead or given away.

"You'll have to eat all those eggs, Margaret," Gerhard teased.

"Oh, I have friends who'll be glad to have them."

"Aren't you staying in Basel?" Gerhard asked in surprise.

"Of course not. I'm following master to Breisgau, though I do dread the trip down the Rhine." She shuddered. "Those green waters rushing by always take my breath away. What if the boat should tip over?"

"You don't go by boat all the way, just to Neuenberg," Gerhard assured her. *Strange,* he thought, *but I don't feel that I'm going with Erasmus.* He couldn't shake off the feeling. What was he going to do, then? Stay in Basel? Where would he live? What would he do? With all the turmoil in Basel, going to the university didn't seem right, even when it started up again, as it surely would. Certainly, Wittenberg University was not the answer. Every idea he thought of seemed to lead to a stone wall. Then somehow he knew he had to go back to his castle, to manage it and the crops, and to do the reading and studying he enjoyed in the big library his father had assembled.

"Going back?" Margaret echoed. "Yes, that seems right for you. You have a duty there."

Was his first duty to have Uncle Frederic arrested for misusing the money from the estate? One of Erasmus' lawyer friends advised Gerhard that this could be done. "Your uncles were only the guardians of the property your parents left you. You are the sole owner of the castle and all its lands. You may prosecute your Uncle Frederic to the full extent of the law."

But the word *prosecute* sounded too much like persecute to Gerhard. There was too much of that everywhere. Besides, Uncle Frederic was converted to the teachings of William Farel. "Don't arrest him," Gerhard told the lawyer. "Let him go his way."

With this decision, Gerhard knew his life would be satisfactory. If only he could have someone to help him, like Andreas, he thought. *I'll manage,* he told himself, and helped Margaret with the boxes for Erasmus' trip.

"Did your friends come after the chickens?" he asked one day.

113

Margaret sniffed. "I never thought it of Master. He knew I had my eye on those chickens."

"What happened to them?"

"Master gave them to the newlyweds," Margaret snapped.

"Who?"

"Justina Froben and her husband, Nicholas Episcopius. They've got my chickens, and I hope they quit laying eggs."

Gerhard burst into laughter. "Is that a Christian way to be?"

"Christian or not, those chickens were like children to me. I do think the master might have given the newlyweds something else. The gold cup Duke George gave him would make a better present." She wound up the final packing in a burst of energy.

The day for Erasmus' departure arrived. He could not ride horseback to the boat landing and two men arrived with a litter. Gerhard, Margaret, and a few friends accompanied him. The men with the litter headed for the town dock.

"No, no, that's too public," Erasmus ordered. "I'll sail from the dock near St. Anthony's."

But the captain of the boat shook his head. "I can't do that."

"Why not?"

"You're too well known to leave from there."

"But no one knows I am leaving," Erasmus said.

The captain smiled. "Sir, I have already been ordered by the city council to prevent you from leaving Basel." As if to prove his words a messenger ran up. "You're wanted at the city hall."

With a glance toward Erasmus, the captain left. He

Two men carried Erasmus to the boat on a litter. Gerhard, Margaret, and a few friends followed along.

came back and was recalled. Two hours went by. On his return this time the captain said, "I have been forbidden to sail from any dock other than the one near the bridge."

Erasmus sighed, waved his hand to the litter men and motioned them toward the municipal dock.

A crowd quickly gathered. "It's Erasmus. He's leaving Basel."

"How long do you plan to stay in Freiburg?" someone asked.

"It is not going to be permanent," Erasmus said.

Typically Erasmian, Gerhard thought.

"I have resolved to remain there this winter," Erasmus went on, "and then to fly with the swallows to the place God calls me." He added, "I am not driven away from Basel. I am going openly."

The captain showed no hurry about leaving.

"What's he waiting for?" the crowd whispered to each other.

"The city council is not going to let Erasmus go."

Margaret fretted about the delay. She would be leaving by a later boat. Friends came up and thanked her for the chickens. Margaret gasped, "But I thought he gave them to someone else." She accepted the thanks and told Gerhard. "Just like the master. Always kind." She found out that Erasmus had written a poem to the newlyweds about the chickens he had intended to send.

After a further delay, with more people gathering, Oecolampadius appeared in great agitation. "Don't go," he implored. "We'll make you a citizen of Basel."

"I prefer to be a citizen of the world," Erasmus replied.

116

"We need you here," Oecolampadius entreated.

"My baggage has already gone on ahead of me," Erasmus said. He took his place in the boat, jotting down a few lines. Oecolampadius came aboard and shook hands with Erasmus, who smiled and thrust a paper toward the minister. As Oecolampadius climbed back to the dock, people asked, "What did Erasmus write?"

It was a poem.

> *And now fair Basel, fare thee well.*
> *These many years to me a host most dear.*
> *All joys be thine, and may Erasmus find*
> *A home as happy as thou gav'st him here.*

"Then why did he leave?" people asked.

"Because of religion," his friends said, claiming that Erasmus had told them so.

On account of the changes in religion, Gerhard told himself weeks later in the castle. In other places people were being exiled, drowned, or persecuted for their beliefs. Louis Berquin was burned at the stake for heresy. How long ago it was, Gerhard reflected, when he had first set out for Basel to meet Erasmus and the two messengers from France had brought the first word of trouble between Berquin and Noel Beda, just one of the many persecutions that were taking place. People's beliefs changed violently, and Gerhard was not really surprised when Andreas appeared at the castle.

"I heard you were here, and I came back. The monastery is not for me."

"Are you still a Catholic, Andreas?"

117

"Yes. Aren't you?"

Gerhard didn't know how to answer at first. "A reformed Catholic."

"Like Erasmus?"

"Call me a Christian," Gerhard said. That was the answer. No other names were necessary. Wasn't that what Erasmus was doing for the world when he laid the egg that Luther hatched?

Louise A. Vernon was born in Coquille, Oregon. Her grandparents crossed the plains in covered wagons as young children.

She earned her BA degree from Willamette University, Salem, Oregon, and studied music at Cincinnati Conservatory. She took advanced studies in music in Los Angeles, after which she turned to Christian journalism. Following three years of special study in creative writing, she began her successful series of religious-heritage juveniles. She teaches creative writing in the San Jose public school district.

Mrs. Vernon re-creates for children the stories of Reformation times and acquaints them with great figures in church history. She has traveled throughout

England and Germany researching firsthand the settings for her stories. In each book she places a child on the scene with the historical character and involves him in an exciting plot.

The National Association of Christian Schools, representing more than 8,000 Christian educators, honored *Ink on His Fingers* as one of the two best children's books with a Christian message released in 1972.

Mrs. Vernon is author of *Peter and the Pilgrims* (early America), *Strangers in the Land* (the Huguenots), *The Secret Church* (the Anabaptists), *The Bible Smuggler* (William Tyndale), *Key to the Prison* (George Fox and the Quakers), *Night Preacher* (Menno Simons and the Anabaptists), *The Beggars' Bible* (John Wycliffe), *Ink on His Fingers* (Johann Gutenberg), *Doctor in Rags* (Paracelsus and the Hutterites), *Thunderstorm in Church* (Martin Luther), *A Heart Strangely Warmed* (John Wesley), and *The Man Who Laid the Egg* (Erasmus).